LOST GIRL VS WOUNDED BOY

FOREVER LOVE #5

JORDAN FORD

NOTE FROM THE AUTHOR

Dear Reader,

I have to be honest and say that this has been the hardest Forever Love novel to write so far. I was really struggling with Stacey and how she was feeling. And then Willow is in a really bad place, but she doesn't know it. As a mother, I've got to admit, it's hard to watch her.

But, as I write this, I realize that ... well, life is messy and confusing sometimes. We don't always know exactly what we want and we're not always aware of everything we're feeling. It's all a process and a journey, and through that struggle we eventually become better versions of ourselves.

So as you journey with these characters, I hope you can see how lost eventually becomes found thanks to good-hearted people and ultimately... love.

And speaking of love, I would like to thank the people who I absolutely love working with…

Rachael, Lenore, Beth, Kristin and Emily. I don't know what I'd do without you guys. You are all talented, thoughtful, beautiful women and it is a privilege to work with you.

To my review team and reader group—I love you guys. Thank you for interacting with me and making this job so enjoyable.

Rose and Greg, thank you for letting me visit your farm and watch you with the calves. It was such a cool experience.

Thank you to my wonderful family, and I want to make special mention to my dad, because he has been the world's best dad. He lives love on a daily basis, and he has taught me so much. I'm very grateful to have him and my amazing mother as role models.

And to my Lord and Savior. Thank you for never leaving my side, for walking every path with me, even when I chose the wrong ones. You are my constant champion, and I love you.

xx

Jordan

THE KIWI DICTIONARY

The Kiwi Dictionary
Haven Bay Series

JORDAN FORD

Every country has their own special lingo and New
Zealand is no exception.
If there are any words or phrases you don't understand,
feel free to download the Kiwi Dictionary. It gets
updated with each new book in the series.
Here's the link:
https://dl.bookfunnel.com/gtguyptohn

1

HAYDEN

T he sun is bright and brilliant, the air just a touch warmer than it has been in a long time. We're ambling around the Hamilton Gardens and the sky is blue, the blossoms are pale pink, the smells in the air are delicious. Spring has begun...

And I'm struggling to enjoy any of it.

I should be the happiest guy on the planet right now. I'm on my first official date with Stacey Freeman. She's looking amazing in her blue skinny jeans with the holes in the knees. She's paired it with a fitted, white cable-knit sweater that matches her Adidas shoes.

Funny thing. We're wearing the same shoes today. It just goes to show how in sync we are. How meant to be we are.

And now I'm dating her.

That's freaking epic!

Stacey Freeman.

She's beautiful, fun, energetic—my favorite person to be around—and now she's my girlfriend. At least I think she is.

She was my best friend, but we've shifted our relationship into the romantic zone, and unfortunately… it's not going so well.

This date needs to be perfect.

I've got a hamper full of food on my back. Shelley, my sister-in-law, helped me put it together. It's all food that should wow and impress. I just hope I haven't forgotten anything.

Aw, man, I can barely think straight, and the nervous energy is making me either talk in high speed or not say anything at all.

Stacey's kind of quiet, which isn't helping either.

I rub my sweaty fingertips together and wonder if I should take her hand. She doesn't really want me doing it at school. After our first kiss a couple of weeks ago, I was kind of hoping that I could swan into school on Monday, capture her hand and we'd be all Stayden or Hacey. But when I appeared by her locker to say good morning, I accidentally scared the crap out of her, and she dropped her book on her toe. It hurt enough for her eyes to water. She swore and jumped around for a minute but then told me not to worry about it.

She probably just said that to stop my incessant string of apologies. I felt so bad. I didn't try touching her again that day, just to be on the safe side. On Tuesday, I was determined not to have a repeat and texted her on the way to her locker so she knew I was coming. She texted back with a *meet me in the music room*.

I wandered down there, kind of perplexed, and sat through this really awkward conversation about how she wants to keep our relationship quiet.

"Quiet?"

"Yeah, like Tane and Harper."

"Tane and Harper are together? I didn't know that."

"Exactly!" She pointed at me, and my guts got this weird concrete kind of feeling, like the blood had stopped flowing through my veins properly.

"So, you don't want people to know we're together?"

She gave me this pained frown. "I just…"

Then Bianca walked in, interrupting us. The bell rang a few minutes later, and I shuffled off, trying to figure out what Stacey really meant.

That night, she sent me a text asking if I'd take her out on a date on Saturday. I was all over it, going into planning mode to prepare something epic for us. But then she had to cancel because she'd completely flaked on a sociology assignment and Beck had told her she wasn't going anywhere until it was finished.

So, here we are now. Another week down the line and our official date is finally happening.

It feels really good, although we should probably talk about the whole secret relationship thing. I don't know if I'm that keen, but I don't want to ruin the moment by getting all serious. The last two weeks have been kind of hard. I feel like one minor mishap just seems to flow into the next. Every conversation at school gets interrupted, and every time I reach for Stacey, something goes wrong.

Our kiss from two weeks ago is almost a distant memory. I haven't managed to make it happen again. But I really want today to change that.

Glancing down at her swinging arm, I hold my breath and capture her hand. She stiffens, then relaxes, smiling at me when I curl my fingers around hers.

That's better.

Holding hands. This is good.

Just breathe, Hayden. It's Stace. Remember? Your bestie.

"So, uh, school holidays next week."

"Yep." Stacey nods.

"Got any plans?"

Oh, this feels so wooden. Why is my voice so tight and pitchy?

"Just this lame camping trip Beck's insisting we go on."

"Oh yeah?" I smile, waiting for her to invite me, but she glances the other way, obviously interested in the English-style garden we're strolling through. The rose-bushes are in bloom and blend perfectly with the white statues mounted on pillars within the symmetrical garden. If I set my mind free, I can almost believe I'm walking the grounds of some English castle.

But my mind's not free.

It's cluttered and pulsing, waiting for those four little words: *Want to join us?*

I frown, wondering if I should mention it, but then that's like super rude to invite yourself to someone else's family thing.

I just figure since I'm her best friend that she'd want me to come along. But maybe now that I'm her boyfriend, things have changed.

Oh shit! Why did I want this?

I pined for her for months before making my move, and ever since, things have just gone from bad to worse.

I miss my bestie. I miss how easy it was to be around her. This whole romance thing is ruining it, but it's what I want, right?

I mean, how many nights does a guy have to dream about a girl to know he's totally crushing on her?

I want this to work.

I want to be her boyfriend.

So, I guess I'll just have to up my game a little.

We walk past a rosebush and I tug Stacey to a stop. She turns to grin at me, and I risk the thorns in order to twist off the prettiest rose of the bunch. It's an effort and I end up cutting my finger, but when I hand it over, her stunning smile tells me she appreciated the effort.

Now would be a great time to kiss her. I move in, ready to tuck my arm around her waist and—

"You're not supposed to pick the flowers."

An indignant little voice makes me turn, and I gaze down to find a small girl with a severe part down the center of her head and two military-tight braids running down each shoulder. Her pudgy little hands are on her hips, and she's frowning at me like I'm some kind of criminal.

"I was just picking my girl—"

"You're not supposed to pick them! Look with your eyes, not your hands." Her face scrunches up, and then she starts wagging her finger at me. "I'm gunna tell."

I kind of don't know what to say to her, but I figure wrapping up this little convo with the Flower Police is for the best. She's just shat all over my romantic moment with Stacey.

Seriously. Can I not catch *one* break?

"Look, I'm sorr—"

"Mummy! Mama!" The little girl spins and starts running toward this gorilla-looking guy and a stern woman pushing a pram.

The little girl is pointing back at me, and I whip around to look at Stacey. I'm completely horrified that I'm getting told on for—

"Off with his head." Stacey puts her finger in the air and starts giggling.

"I know, right?" I start laughing too, until she gasps and points over my shoulder.

The family is now heading toward us.

"Oh, crud."

"Run!" Stacey snatches my hand and starts tugging me out of the English garden. Her laughter is only getting harder, which is making me crack up too, and our running is basically hopeless—flailing limbs and stumbling feet. We keep loping along, jumping around people and chortling as we escape the mini Queen of Hearts.

We round the corner into the hippie-style garden, getting curious frowns and glances as we cavort around in hysterics. Our legs are rubber, our idiotic laughter uncontrollable.

Stumbling past the veggies, we bust out into the herb garden and I collide directly with a pram, flipping over the front wheel and landing in the dirt with a crash.

Small, sharp stones dig into the palms of my hands as I sort of control my fall, but my face still gets smothered in dust. Rolling onto my back, I hiss at the spots of pain radiating through different parts of my body. My knee where I clipped the pram, my grazed palms, my protesting elbow.

"What the hell do you think you're doing?" the father starts yelling at me. "Watch it! My kid's in there."

"Sorry, sir." I spit the dirt from my mouth and start wiping my dusty lips.

Stacey's still giggling behind me.

"This is no laughing matter," the man barks. "You two are being inconsiderate and dangerous."

I get back to my feet, brushing the grime off my pants and trying to ignore the sting in my elbow. I've definitely grazed it. Stacey is biting her lips together, and her cheeks are going a little red as she stares down at the ground in front of us.

"Get out of here!" The man points toward the exit, and we shuffle off, our laughter instantly tamed by the irate father. Every eyeball in the herb garden follows our trail.

It's so embarrassing.

I can't believe it. Two minutes of utter joy and I had to go and ruin it by assing over and endangering a baby.

This is the worst. Stacey's never going to say yes to another date again!

2

STACEY

Aw, man, I can't believe that just happened.

Dipping my head, I adjust my shades and pick up my pace, desperate to get out of the herb garden as quickly as possible.

I hate the *all eyes on me* sensation. Their stares feel like laser beams trying to drill holes into my back.

And just when we were having so much fun too.

Hayden's gone really quiet beside me.

"Are you hurt?" I ask him.

"Not really." He shakes his head and musters a smile that barely moves his mouth. "Let's just find somewhere quiet to eat."

"Okay," I whisper and follow him.

I've only been to the Hamilton Gardens once before,

and I don't really know my way around. Hayden doesn't try taking my hand or anything; we just quietly shuffle to a nice, open green patch near the playground.

"Let's go on this side." Hayden points through an archway, and we leave the happy squeals of little kids behind us and find a spot under a big leafy tree.

Gazing behind me, a memory flashes through my brain. It was dark, and the squeals from the playground weren't little kids but teenage idiots. Idiots I thought were cool and wanted to be my friends. People I trusted. Trusted with all of me.

The burn marks Jonas left behind still itch and hurt when I think about it. Plunking down onto the picnic blanket, I rub my arms, trying to ward off the dark memories, so relieved Hayden knows nothing about them.

All I've told him is that my ex slept with me and then dumped me the next day. I'll never admit to the video I didn't know was being recorded or how it was posted online for the world to see. I just pray Hayden never stumbles across it. I mean, it's offline now, but rumors and stories last forever. It could get to him one day. All I can hope is that he'll never believe it. I'll deny it black and blue if he ever asks me about it. I know it's bad to lie, but he can't know what Jonas did to me. He just can't.

A couple walks past us, strolling along, hand in hand.

The big guy glances at our picnic spot, his gaze lingering over me for what feels like a second too long. I look away from him, hoping I'm just imagining it, haunted yet again by the questions: How many people saw me naked? How many people have seen me lose my virginity?

The police took the video down as soon as possible, but it was up for about a week.

A week.

A lot of people can see a video clip in one week.

I shudder and grip my elbows.

"You cold?" Hayden starts shrugging out of his varsity-style jacket.

I'm not really, but I don't want to admit why I'm shaking. I also don't want him getting cold. He's not exactly a big guy, and there isn't much fat on him to insulate his body.

"That's okay, you don't—"

But he's already arranging the jacket around my shoulders. It's sweet, and I don't want to ruin the moment.

Since impulsively kissing him at my family's midwinter celebration, I feel like I've cursed our friendship. I can't tell him this, of course, but ever since I made that move, I can't shake the feeling that it was the wrong one.

I like Hayden.

JORDAN FORD

He's such a great guy, but were we better off as friends?

I don't know if I'm ready for romance again, but I've kissed him now, and I don't want to hurt his feelings. He's a really great kisser too, not that we've done it much. Things keep getting in the way, and I so don't want to go public at school. There's been enough gossip about me as it is. I don't want to ignite more by walking through the school holding Hayden's hand.

I hate to think what people might imagine about us.

When will they be recording a sex tape?

I thought he was gay? Why is Stacey dating him?

Stacey and Hayden? What a joke!

Ugh!

As much as I want everyone to think how cool it is that I'm dating the world's sweetest guy, I just know they won't.

People feed off the negatives. They make assumptions and see what they want to see.

Nasty comments continue to swirl through my brain no matter how hard I try to ignore them. I just don't want to go there. I want to keep flying below the radar, which is weird for me. I used to love the spotlight. I used to be so confident and sure of myself. Guys checking me out empowered me. I said what I wanted. I thrived on the drama.

I kind of miss that girl, but I don't know how to get her back... or if I even want her back.

Look where cocky blindness got me last time.

This heavy feeling I can't explain sloshes around in my stomach. I don't remember drinking petrol for breakfast, but my guts are full of it.

"Okay, so today on the menu, we have…" Hayden starts presenting each item of the picnic like he's the new host of a cooking show.

He definitely has flare. The guy wants to be a hairstylist, but I think acting or presenting would totally work for him too. He can be so dramatic and flamboyant when he wants to be.

I bet he's doing it to try and make up for what just happened. He wants to see me smile again, hear my laugh. Poor guy. He's still got a little dirt smeared on his cheek, and his sandy blond hair will need a good wash tonight. I kind of don't want to tell him that, because hair is really important to him, and he'd hate to see the state his is in right now.

Aw, his poor hands. I can see a little graze on the heel of one of them. He's done pretty well covering up the pain of hurtling over a pram and landing in the dirt.

Laugh, Stace. Make him feel better.

I force one out, really going for a genuine giggle when

he presents the bunch of grapes and singsongs, "Nature's candy."

He grins and lays out this platter of nibbles—soft cheese and crackers, salami, hummus, dips, olives, dates, grapes. It looks amazing, and it's obvious he's gone to a lot of effort. It's really sweet.

"And some bubbles." He pulls out a bottle of sparkling grape juice, and I grin as he wrestles with the cork.

"Here, I'll do it."

"No, I've got it." He grunts, struggling to pop the cork free.

It eventually fires out, hitting me right in the shoulder.

"Ow." I slap my hand over the sting, and Hayden goes beet red.

"I'm sorry."

He looks about ready to cry, and I shake my head.

"No big deal." Rubbing my shoulder, I ignore the slight pain and reach for the two plastic wineglasses he packed in the bag.

"I'm so sorry."

"Hayden, it's fine. Seriously. It doesn't hurt. I just said 'ow' because it surprised me. That's all." I keep smiling until he believes me, then stick out my glass. "Bubble me up."

He pours the drink, the bottle shaking just a little. He's looking kind of morose as he settles the bottle back into the bag and sips his drink.

Oh, man. This is turning out to be such a disaster. Why is this happening to us? We're usually so good together. It's easy to be around him. Comfortable. Relaxing.

Because he was my bestie.

Is my bestie.

Crap! I don't know what he is now.

I sip on the fizzy grape juice and steal a sideways glance at him. Should I say something to lighten the moment? But what?

Argh! This is such hard work.

The thwack of a boot hitting a soccer ball catches my attention, and I turn to watch it sail through the air. It lands near us and keeps rolling, three boys and a girl chasing after it. She's fast and gets to the ball first, flicking it with her foot before dribbling it away from us. She's pretty good for what, an eight- or nine-year-old?

I can't stop watching her as she totally outplays at least two of the boys. Her main competition is a taller kid who looks to be her older brother maybe? They have pretty similar features.

Her blonde hair flies as she chases after the ball,

laughing with glee when she reaches it first and, with some skillful footwork, gets around her brother.

She reminds me of me a little. I couldn't sit still when I was her age. I was always wanting to run, play, jump, throw, handstand, skip, twirl—anything to keep my body moving.

Now...

Rubbing my fingers together, I fight the urge to jump up and join them.

I kind of gave up sport after Mum and Dad died. I'm not even sure why. Maybe it's because it was something I shared with Mum and the idea of doing it without her was just too painful. Jonas wasn't into sport, and I got caught up with his crowd, and I don't know...

Do I miss it?

As I watch the girl in front of me messing around with the soccer ball, a resounding YES echoes through my brain.

Doing the cross-country last week was pretty fun. I really enjoyed that. Hayden and I loped around together. He's a good long-distance runner. We didn't place or anything, but we would have easily been in the top twenty.

I wonder what he's like with other sporty stuff.

Resting my hand back on the picnic rug, I start to

imagine joining in with the kids in front of us and a smile twitches my lips.

I'm so lost in the idea that when Hayden brushes his fingers over mine, I actually jump with fright, spilling grape juice down my sweater.

Crap. Why did I have to wear white today?

I snatch a napkin out of the basket and start mopping it up.

"Sorry, I didn't mean to scare you." Hayden gives me a pained frown.

I ball up the sodden napkin and throw it in the basket. Poor Hayden. He looks so sad and hurt. I reach for his hand and force what I hope looks like a genuine smile. "I was just lost in thought."

"About what?"

I chuckle and shake my head. "Nothing."

"You can tell me. You can tell me anything."

With a thick swallow, I grab a grape and pop it in my mouth so I don't have to answer him.

An awkward silence falls between us, and I look back to the soccer kids, trying to figure out what to do next. Maybe we should ask to play. We're obviously not doing great on the talking front right now, so why don't we jump up and do something active?

I whip back to suggest it, not realizing that Hayden is leaning in at the same time. Our foreheads crack together, pain radiating behind my eyes.

"Ow," Hayden murmurs, covering his eyebrow and muttering something under his breath.

This is unbelievable. Seriously. Could this date get any worse?

We should never have left the friend zone. This isn't working.

Why am I always so damn impulsive? Why'd I have to kiss him and then tell him that I like him as more than a friend?

Do I really want this?

Maybe. I mean, it's Hayden. He's sweet and kind and funny.

I just—

The soccer ball comes flying toward us, and I quickly snatch it before it can hit Hayden in the head. The kids run up to our picnic spot, obviously expecting me to throw the ball back and maybe bark at them to be a little more careful.

Instead I smile and ask, "Hey, can we play?"

The kids look at each other, comically mystified, but then they all start nodding. I jump up with a grin and flick my hand at Hayden. "Come on!"

He gives me a doubtful frown before getting off the picnic blanket and reluctantly trailing me onto the grass. I drop the ball and give it a light boot to the girl, who dribbles it up the field. I stay with her, securing the ball when it comes to me and weaving around the guys who I think love having a couple of older people to compete with.

It ends up turning into a super fun game of soccer.

Hayden's pretty good and gets a goal early on.

"Score!" he screeches, punching his hands in the air and doing a little happy dance.

The girl beside me giggles while her older brother cringes and scratches the back of his neck. I don't know why his reaction bothers me so much. He's a kid I don't even know, but something about that look on his face makes me realize how people see Hayden sometimes.

How they'll see me if they know I'm dating him.

3

WILLOW

I pull the sheet up a little higher, tucking it around my chest to secure it. I don't want anyone walking in and seeing me naked.

To be honest, I kind of want to get dressed, but when I moved to grab my clothes before, Heath snatched my arm and yanked me against him.

"Not yet. Please. Not just yet." The smile in his dark blue eyes stopped me, and I nestled against his bare chest, loving the strength of it, relishing the sensation of his fingers lightly trailing down my bare back.

But then he moved to grab himself a cigarette, and now I'm sitting next to him, worrying that one of his friends might walk in at any moment and know what we've been up to. I mean, they probably already do. When we first arrived at Heath's friend's place, he led me through the throng of people, past the speakers that were vibrating with music and up to the owner.

"Got a spare room?"

"You can use mine." The guy chuckled, wiggling his eyebrows as he took a swig from his beer bottle and checked me out.

I flushed and squeezed Heath's hand, happy to be getting away from the curious glances. Heath and I don't hang out with his friends too often. We usually like to be alone.

Which I guess we kind of are, if you forget about the party people outside the door.

I focus on the thump of the music pulsing through the house and reach for my vodka and lemon mixer. This is the only alcohol I like the taste of. Heath made me try a whole bunch, and I finally settled on these, so he buys them for me all the time. He's old enough, and I kind of love that. I'm not just dating some stupid high school boy. I'm dating a man.

A sales rep for a beverage company I can never remember the name of. He owns a flash car, wears a suit to work and can buy me drinks that help me relax. I've got it made.

A stream of smoke oozes between Heath's lips. I watch it rise into the air, not loving the smell, but I'm not about to dump the guy because he's a smoker.

LOST GIRL VS WOUNDED BOY

He passes me the cigarette and I take it, because I know he prefers it when I have a few puffs with him. I inhale the smallest amount and quickly blow it back out before it can hit the back of my throat. Gulping down another mouthful of vodka lemon, I swish the smoky taste away and smile at my boyfriend.

He smirks at me, and I'm taken back to the first moment I saw him.

I was sitting on April's bed, waiting for her to get us some snacks from the kitchen when Heath walked past the door. He doubled back and introduced himself. I was still learning to find my voice again at that point, so I didn't say much, but he didn't seem to mind. He was friendly and nice to me.

He's a good-looking guy—dark, slicked-back hair and a strong, clean-shaven face that always smells of delicious cologne. He has a great sense of style too, with his various shirts and ties. He wears those shiny shoes with the really pointed toes as well. I love those.

But it's not just that. He has this perpetual presence about him, this spark in his eyes that I'm drawn to.

He asked me my name, and I managed to whisper, "Willow."

He gave me this awestruck stare like I was the most beautiful thing he'd ever seen. "That's a pretty name… for a pretty girl."

My heart did a complete three-sixty. I could feel it swelling and pulsing while butterflies danced through my body, their delicate wings tickling all the right parts of me until I let out a soft giggle.

Then April came back into the room and told Heath to get out.

"We've talked about this! It's my space. My room! Get out!"

"Just meeting your friend," he said pleasantly.

"Don't. She's *my* friend."

It was totally awkward, and Heath slipped out of the room. April was kind of steaming and muttered something about annoying brothers. "He thinks he owns this place. It drives me crazy. I wish he hadn't moved back home."

I quietly shared the food with her but couldn't stop checking the door to see if Heath would walk past again. I didn't see him, but I found every excuse in the book to keep hanging out with April at her place. Every time I went over, I'd look for Heath, and sometimes I'd be lucky enough to find him.

He'd talk to me, tell me something funny, and I'd find myself reliving the little conversations, dreaming about him at night. One time he brushed his hand down my arm, and I felt this electricity race through me. It was an addictive feeling, and I started to crave it.

He must have too, because the next time, he snuck me his phone number. "Don't tell anyone I've given you this. It can be our little secret."

I love that. There's something so thrilling about being in a hidden relationship.

Heath has switched something on inside of me, and the yearning is overpowering.

We've been secretly dating for nearly two months, although April knows about it now. She walked into the bathroom one afternoon and found Heath and me kissing. She wasn't that happy, but it was kind of a relief. Hiding it from her was getting harder and harder. Plus, I need her help in order to see Heath.

April hates it, so I came up with the idea of using ballet as a front. It keeps Harper happy and out of my hair too. So, now I spend my school days with April, and the odd weekend, just to keep her happy, and I spend every ballet lesson with Heath.

It's a good arrangement, and now that I've upped 'dancing' to four times a week, it's even better. Heath will drop anything to be with me. He skips out on work to come and collect me. He's always there for me. Our relationship has been fast and intense, but I wouldn't have it any other way. He's brought me to life in this powerful way, and I'm kind of addicted to the feeling.

His solid hand slips beneath the sheets and runs down my thigh, giving it a suggestive squeeze before heading north. My stomach pinches. We've already had sex once this afternoon. Does he really want to do it again already? Can't we just snuggle?

I glance at his face, noting the hunger in his eyes, and resolve myself to the inevitable. Thankfully sex never takes very long, and he always holds me afterward, telling me he loves me. That's the part I live for. Heath starts kissing my neck, and I'm trying to psych myself up for it when my phone dings.

"I better check it." I jump at the interruption and roll away to grab the phone. Heath trails his fingers down my shoulder and arm, kissing the back of my neck while my heart does an uncomfortable jolt.

April: Ballet class ends in fifteen minutes. You better be there or Harper might go in looking for you.

I gasp and check the time. "Ballet's finishing soon."

Heath jerks and looks over my shoulder at the text. "Shit, already? Why didn't my alarm go off?" He rolls away from me, checking his phone before pushing me out of the bed. "I thought I'd set it! Shit! Hurry up. Get dressed."

I flop onto the floor, scrambling to my feet and snatching my pale pink ballet tights. Bunching them up, I glance at Heath and notice he's stopped moving in order to check me out. He smirks at me, his eyebrows rising just a little. I blush, loving the expression on his face. He always makes me feel so pretty.

He takes a slow drag from his cigarette before squishing the rest into an ashtray by the bed. I wrestle my tights on and grab my leotard, unearthing an empty condom packet. I cringe and quickly throw it in the bin. Imagine if his friend walked in and found it on the floor. How embarrassing. It definitely feels weird having sex in the guy's bed, but Heath and I don't have a place of our own. It's not like we can go to April's house when she's home, and there's no way my family can ever find out about Heath.

We usually hit isolated trails and parks in the area, but today this place was free. It was nice to do it in a bed for a change.

My hands shake as I wrestle my hair into a bun.

"Do it in the car. Can't be late. Don't want to get busted." Heath grabs my wrist and pulls me out the door. It hurts a little. He has no idea how strong his grip is. I'm just about to wriggle free when he lets me go and wraps his arm around me, securely leading me out of the house. I love this feeling.

We weave through the party and finally step into the fresh air. The foul-smelling smoke we busted through at the end was disgusting. It smelled different to the cigarettes I share with Heath. Like dog poo or something super gross.

I wrinkle my nose as I slip into Heath's Skyline. It's a total boy racer car that he bought cheap and got his mate to do up for him. I love his cobalt blue car. It's super sexy, just like Heath.

I grin as he speeds to ballet and parks around the corner in our usual spot. Before I can even reach for the handle, he cups the back of my head and pulls me in for a passionate kiss that awakens all of me.

Dammit. Why does ballet have to end so soon?

"See you tomorrow," he whispers before handing me a piece of gum.

I pop it into my mouth. "Love you."

"You too." He kisses me again, and I reluctantly get out of the car, watching him pull away and speed off down the street.

My body feels like it's on fire as I rush back to the old church, which has been transformed into a ballet school. I go to my usual spot on the curb, just down from the school. I told Harper it was easier to collect me from there, less busy, which is true and exactly what I need. I don't want the students leaving the school and giving me odd looks wondering why I'm dressed for class but not actually attending it.

I struggle with a bobby pin, trying to straighten up my

hair and make it look neat and tidy before Harper arrives. She's got eyes like a freaking hawk. I chew my gum a little harder, needing to eradicate the smell of liquor and cigarettes.

I highly doubt my sister would be cool with me drinking, smoking and dating a guy who's five years older than me.

She wouldn't even give me a chance to explain how much I love Heath and how much he's done for me, so there's no point even starting the conversation. The secrecy is there to protect us, and it just adds another thrill to what we're doing.

I haven't felt that kind of energy ever.

Glancing over my shoulder, I glimpse the ballet school and for a brief moment wonder if I *have* actually felt that energy before. But in a different way. I was a pretty good dancer. Being on stage and moving my body like that was awesome, empowering even. But I don't... When my parents died, I felt this weird sense of liberation. I danced for them. They loved ballet so much and were so proud of me, always telling their friends about me and how good I was. Now that they're gone, I don't feel that pressure to do it anymore.

I'm free.

No more perfect pirouettes required.

I don't know how to feel about that.

Sometimes I almost want to let out this carefree laugh, but it always turns to ash in my mind, because it means they're not here anymore. Dad will never watch me dance again, never admire me from the audience, never drive me to another lesson, never ask me to explain what all those French words mean. I can't stand it.

As much as I don't miss the rigid structure of ballet, I miss *him*.

More than anything.

Our family wagon appears around the corner and I paste on a smile, shifting into happy Willow mode because that's the one Harper likes best. As soon as she stops the car, I slip into the backseat.

"You want to sit in the front?"

"No, I'm good. You can be my chauffeur." The joke will get me out of having to explain that I smell a little smoky. The farther I sit from her, the better.

"So, how was the double class today? You must be exhausted."

"Yeah, it was really good. Super fun. I am a little tired, though. My body feels like jelly." I keep going, rehashing stories from the ballet I did in Wellington. Harper won't have heard them because she didn't collect me from ballet. She had her own life, was busy with her friends. It was Dad who was my chauffeur. Dad who I'd sit next to.

Dad.

My chest starts to hurt, my eyeballs aching as I gaze out the window and remember the details of my father's face. His adoring eyes. That sweet smile. His neatly styled hair and perfectly knotted ties. His Omega watch that was always set to the right time.

Closing my eyes, I try to replace that sadness with images of Heath. His intense gaze, the pads of his fingers igniting my skin, the wild thrill of doing things I know I shouldn't.

My heart starts racing, and as soon as I get home, I haul my butt up to the shower so I can hide the smell of my afternoon tryst with flowery shampoo and shower gel.

As the hot water hits my skin and I lather my body, I start to relax. It's always a tense trip home, wondering if I'll let something slip, but today was another success.

I can't help a triumphant smirk in the mirror as I comb out my long, straight hair. It's the same color as Dad's. I go still, gazing at my reflection until my phone buzzes on the bathroom counter.

April: Did you make it in time?

Me: Yes.

· · ·

April: Nice of you to let me know. Thanks.

I cringe, April's sarcasm feeling like a slap to the face. I'll have to make it up to her tomorrow. She's a good friend, and I enjoy hanging out with her. I really need to keep her on my side if I'm going to keep this thing with Heath going.

He's the first boyfriend I've ever had. The first guy I've ever loved.

I can't lose him.

I can't go back to the way things were before. That cold isolation, the constant gray fog rolling inside of me, stealing my voice. Heath brought me back to life when no one else could.

I need him.

4

HAYDEN

The trip home from Hamilton Gardens is a quiet one. Usually we'd be singing along to the radio or the awesome Spotify playlist I especially curated for this date, but not right now. I mean, the music is still playing, but we're not singing.

Stacey's quiet.

It's eerie and I hate it, but I don't know what to say.

This date has not gone at all how I planned it. My eyebrow is still kind of tender from where we smacked heads, but I'm doing my best not to touch it. I was leaning in to try and kiss her, or whisper something in her ear to make her smile. I can't even think what it was now, but my plan was to whisper something nice and then hopefully score myself a kiss.

I'm such an idiot.

Like she'd want to kiss me after I hit her with a bottle cork and then made her spill grape juice all over her white sweater.

I roll my eyes and shake my head. Hopefully months or maybe years down the track, we'll look back on this day and laugh. If we get months or years. I wouldn't be surprised if she wanted to call it quits after this.

Gripping the wheel, I clench my jaw and pull up at the end of Stacey's driveway. "I can take you up to the house if you want, but I know you're wanting to keep us on the down-low."

Stacey glances at me, her smile unreadable. Is it sad? Resigned? What?

"You're still my best friend, and they all know that." Her blue eyes almost glitter, and I lean across the car, slowly, cautiously, hoping for the best. I don't want to smack heads again or scare her, but I also don't want to be shoved back in the friend zone so easily.

Gently tracing the shape of her face with my finger, I try to figure out what she's thinking. I always thought dating my best friend would be the ultimate.

But…

"Sorry the date was such a disaster."

Stacey giggles. "It wasn't all bad, and the soccer was pretty fun."

Yeah, fun, but not romantic.

I purse my lips, wondering if I should say that or simply write off this day and start afresh tomorrow. "You wanna hang out tomorrow? I can find us somewhere secret to go." I trail my fingers down her arm and wriggle my eyebrows, hoping for a laugh.

Instead she watches them in silence until I reach her wrist. Her swallow is thick and foreboding. "Uh, yeah, um… I'm not sure. I'll have chores and stuff since I skipped out on today, so…"

I nod, desperately trying to hide my disappointment. "That's cool. I guess I'll see you on Monday at school."

She smiles and I drink it in, trying to make it warm me. It doesn't have the same effect as usual. I'm cold, because I can feel the inevitable brewing. I want this so badly to work, but—

"Thanks for understanding about the secrecy thing."

I smile, thinking, *I don't, actually!* But I don't say it. This date's gone bad enough; I don't want to make it worse.

Should I kiss her?

Would that make the ending good or bad?

Does she want me to?

I lean forward, then back, hesitating over what to do. Stacey laughs, then rests her hand on my shoulder, lightly pecking my lips.

"See ya later… bestie." And with that she jumps out of the car.

I stay put, watching her walk up the driveway.

She turns once to wave goodbye and blow me another kiss. I catch it and rub it into my cheek, which makes her laugh before she spins and keeps walking.

I take my cue and drive home. Mum's little Mini practically takes me there on autopilot. I really love that she left me her car. She always loved this thing, and now I get to drive it. I can still see her in here, chatting away while she drove me to cricket practice or the mall.

We could talk about anything. She knew me better than anyone on this entire planet.

I miss her.

I wish cancer wouldn't kill people.

I wish I had more than this car and her letters to me.

If only she were here right now, she'd be able to tell me what to do.

She always had the best advice. I know that's rare. Parents always have advice, and most of the time you don't bother taking it, but Mum was someone I could listen to. I trusted her.

"Mum," I whisper, sucking in a ragged breath. "Please, what do I do?"

5

WILLOW

I purse my lips as I reread the text conversation I've just had with April. My frown is so deep it's actually hurting my forehead. I don't know what I'm supposed to do right now.

April: Why does Heath always get the weekends? I wanted to go shopping with you today.

Me: Maybe I can tell Harper that you'll pick me up and we can hang out after ballet.

April: If Heath hears you've done that, he'll just want to keep you with him for longer. Forget it. I'll see you at school.

. . .

I drop my phone with a sigh, running my hands through my hair and starting to gather it into a tight bun. Maybe I can ask Heath to hang out at his place this afternoon, and then I'll surprise April. She'll be stoked. That way I'm spending time with both of them.

Snatching the bobby pins off my nightstand, I start shoving them in. Running to the bathroom, I quickly check that my hair is ballet perfect before grabbing my pale pink pointe shoes and shoving them into the bag with the rest of my gear.

I so don't miss wearing these things. They hurt my toes. Every single time.

"You're so elegant on that stage, Princess. Like a fairy queen. Shakespeare's own Titania." I squeeze my eyes shut, desperate to avoid full-blown demolition. But Dad's proud smile sticks to the edges of my mind no matter how hard I try.

"I don't want that," I mutter. "I want Heath."

I focus back on my boyfriend, convincing myself he won't mind the slight change of plans. He'll get that April's my friend and I need to spend time with her too. Man, I can't wait to get my driver's license. Everything will be a million times easier when I can just take a car and be vague about where I'm going. Not being restricted will mean I can give Heath the time he wants and still appease April with a shopping trip. I've already started studying the road code, and as soon as I turn sixteen in a few weeks, I'm going for my learner's test so I can get this driving thing underway.

Trotting down the stairs, I hunt for my older sister and find her staring at the computer in Beck's office.

"Are you ready? I don't want to be late."

Harper glances over her shoulder. She's frowning, and I so hope it's something to do with accounts for the farm and not me. Closing the screen window, she grabs a sheet of paper off the desk and hands it to me as she walks out the door. "This is really weird. Your ballet school still hasn't charged me for those extra classes you've started taking." With an irritated tut, she slides her shades on while I stare at the invoice for one ballet lesson a week and try to stop the paper from shaking. "Yet another thing I have to follow up on. I'll give them a call tomorrow to sort it out."

My heart is going to explode… and not in a good way.

"Don't do that," I snap, rushing out the door after her. "I'll talk to the office lady at my Tuesday class."

"But—"

"She won't be there today. It's the weekend. But she'll be in on Tuesday, and I can ask her about it then."

"It'll only take me a few minutes to call her."

I huff, panic trying to choke me as I struggle to fold the invoice in half. "But I just said I can talk to her!" I flick my arm in the air. "I'm sixteen in less than three weeks. These are *my* classes, and I need to take responsibility for them." Harper opens her mouth to say something, and I quickly snap, "You're not my mother, okay? I can do this."

Harper's mouth slowly shuts and she nods, whispering a soft "Okay then" before slipping into the car.

She doesn't say much on the journey to the studio, which is a huge relief. It gives me a chance to think about how I'm going to solve this major problem. I've got to figure out a way to divert this whole paying for extra classes thing. I should have considered it before telling Harper I'd signed up for extra lessons.

Pulling up to the curb, she turns to smile at me. "What time's pickup?"

"I'm going shopping with April after class, so I'll get her dad to drop me home."

"Okay." Harper looks out the windscreen, a muscle in her jaw working for a second, before she turns back to me and softly says, "You need to be home for dinner. It's a school night, so... can you make sure April's dad drops you back by six?"

I roll my eyes.

"I know I'm not your parent, but I'm just saying what Mum and Dad would have. Trying to be consistent, that's all."

I don't say anything. My voice always disappears when she brings up our parents. Everything disappears, like my ability to open the car door and make a jump for freedom.

"I'm still not allowed to come in and watch, am I?" Harper tries to smile, obviously hating my silence. "Just for like two minutes?"

Panic jolts my voice box into action and I shake my head, hoping I sound light and breezy. "You know how strict they are. It's just like it was in Wellington."

My sister sighs and nods, then gives me a watery smile. "I'm really proud of you, Will. I know it took a lot of courage to start dancing again. I think it's amazing that you are."

I feel like I've just swallowed a handful of pebbles. My lips are heavy as I force them into a smile. "Thanks."

I can't tell her. She thinks I love ballet as much as Mum and Dad did. How do I say, "I'm not missing it," without implying that I don't miss them either? It's too complicated to try and explain.

Scrambling for the door handle, I tumble out of the car and walk toward the building, the wind tugging at my clothing as I hope Harper takes off before I reach the old church. She's watching me; I can feel it. Turning around, I lift my arm and wave at her.

"Love you," I shout, hoping it's enough to get her on her way.

She beeps a couple of times and pulls into the traffic. It's not until her car has disappeared down the road that my body starts to relax. The muscles that were about to snap unwind as I walk around the back of the building and find Heath leaning against the old fence where he usually is.

With a little giggle, I run into his arms and he lifts me off my feet. I wrap my legs around his waist, and he spins me once before starting to walk for his car. He's in his casual wear today—faded jeans and his favorite *I am a Legend* T-shirt. I love that he looks cool in anything he wears. He knows how to dress like a superstar... just like my dad did.

I shove the thought aside and cling a little tighter. I'm his spider monkey, kissing his neck and loving the strength of his arms holding me tightly against him.

Once we reach his car, he plunks me down and presses me against the window, his lips hot and hungry. "How long have I got you for?"

"It's a one-hour class," I murmur between kisses, "but I told Harper that I'm shopping with April afterward, so I'm not due home until six."

"Excellent." He grins, opening the door for me.

I wait until he's slipped into his own seat before softly

saying, "I thought I probably should go and spend some time with April, so after we've hung out for a bit, can we go back to your place?"

Heath frowns and slams his door shut.

I swallow, wondering if I should say anything as he starts the car and punches away from the curb. "She gets you all week at school. The weekends are mine."

"I know. I just… She wanted to go shopping, and we can't do that during school time."

"Why not? I used to skip out all the time. It's no big deal."

"Yeah." I nod, not willing to tell him that I think it is kind of a big deal. "But April—"

"Is a goody-goody who is petrified of ever putting one toe out of line." He scoffs and shakes his head.

He doesn't get snippy like this very often, but I don't like it when he does.

I lick my bottom lip and try to soothe him. I don't want to waste our precious time together fighting. "I didn't tell her that I was free today. I was gunna surprise her, so…"

Heath slows at the lights and looks over at me, his expression softening. Taking my hand, he gently kisses my palm. Happiness travels through my body. I love the look on his face right now. "I just want to be with you so much. I miss you during the week. All I get is two ballet lessons, and the rest of the time I'm pining for you until the weekend rolls around. I don't want to have to share you."

Aw. How sweet is that?

My heart's a piece of putty as I grin at him. "You don't have to share me."

"Excellent." He smirks and takes a left, driving us to a quiet spot near the lake. It's really secluded behind these two massive willow trees. We've parked here before, and I know exactly what I'll be doing this afternoon. We'll work our way through a few bottles, smoke a couple of ciggies and no doubt have sex. That seems to be Heath's favored routine. We've only been sleeping together for a couple of weeks, but now that we've done it once, he seems to want to do it all the time.

I tuck my hands under my legs and gaze out the window. I shouldn't be complaining about it. It's nice to be wanted. Loved. Spending time with Heath is great. It's liberating. I don't have to point my toe a certain way, keep my torso strong and straight. I'm not striving for the perfect arabesque or grand jeté.

Heath's not asking me to talk about my feelings or open up about the constant pain in my heart. All I have to do is listen to him tell me about his work and the stuff he's into, and then kiss him, cuddle him and lie underneath him. It's easy, really.

Biting my lips together, I swallow to counter the ache in my throat.

I'm lucky.

Not all girls have a boyfriend they can count on.

But I have one who will drop anything to spend time with me. He loves me so much he doesn't even want to share me with his sister.

6

STACEY

The calving stalls are kind of smelly today, but I'd rather be in here feeding these cuties than out there in the wind. It's really blustery outside, and I'm already looking forward to getting back to the house for a hot shower and... homework, of all things.

Seriously, what is wrong with me?

I'm looking *forward* to doing homework.

I roll my eyes, wondering who the hell I am these days.

I think it's more just wanting to get it off my plate so I can relax over the holidays. Only one week to go until two weeks of freedom.

Bianca appears in the barn door, humming cheerfully as she clumps across to me.

"What are you doing here?" I grunt, struggling to move a stubborn calf that needs to feed.

Bianca climbs into the pen and gives me a hand. "I don't have anything else to do."

We wrestle the calf over to the drinking trough and find a free teat for her to suck on.

"Come on, girl," Bianca coaxes her. "You can do it."

I shove my finger in the calf's mouth to get it open, and she takes the teat. "Suck. That's all you gotta do."

It takes two more attempts, but finally the little calf is sucking on the milk, her tail wagging like crazy.

Bianca and I grin at each other, then move to the other pen to get started on those calves.

"I thought you'd be with Cam today."

"He's doing some family time." Bianca's forehead wrinkles.

I don't know every detail, but I know enough. Cam's dad has been a struggling alcoholic for years—on and off the drink as he's tried to control it but constantly failed. A couple of weeks ago, he completely lost it and ended up taking it out on Cam. Bianca's boyfriend was a mess, and he'd had enough. He told it to his dad straight, that he needed to get some proper help this time.

"The rehab not going well?" I tentatively ask. It's a touchy subject. Cam doesn't like anyone knowing about it, but we all saw his face, and Bianca whispered the truth to me as we lay in our dark room together, then made me promise I'd never tell anyone outside of the family.

I did. It was an easy promise to make. Cam's protected me as best he can from the sex movie rumors circulating at school. I'm pretty sure I'd do anything for the guy. He's good all the way through to his core.

"It's going okay, but I think it's pretty tough. His dad is having to go to counseling sessions every day, but his work was nice enough to give him compassionate leave, so that's good."

"How's Cam coping with it all?"

"He hates it. His mum is super fragile over everything, from burnt toast to the toilet not flushing properly. She actually cried the other day when the toilet wouldn't stop running. All she had to do was give the button a little jiggle, but she totally broke down over it. I think deep down, she's freaking out that her husband is going to leave her or something, like if he's totally sober, he might not want her around anymore. She probably needs counseling too. Cam really needs a break from it all. I'm so glad we're going camping this coming weekend."

I grunt, completely unimpressed by the fact that we are.

Honestly! Who goes camping in the winter? Well, spring, but it's only just. It's still freaking cold!

I shove a calf onto a free teat and stand close by until it's sucking properly, then point at the calf closest to Bianca. "That one needs putting back on."

She helps it out, her soft voice gently encouraging the little thing to start drinking. It's so funny watching them all. Personalities shine through pretty quickly. The strong ones are in there, guzzling all the milk before the meek, skinny ones can even get to the drinking trough.

"So, have you invited Hayden yet?" Bianca strokes the calf's head. "You better get on with it. He'll need time to prepare."

Groan! Why did she have to ask?

I go for a casual shrug and move into the third and final pen, my floral gumboots slapping onto the ground when I land. "Yeah, I don't know."

"You don't know? What do you mean?"

"About inviting him. Camping's probably not even his thing."

"Stace, seriously?" Bianca lands beside me in the hay, her expression incredulous. "You're not inviting him? Why not?"

"I just..." I shrug.

"He's your best friend."

"Yeah, kind of."

"Kind of? Have you guys had a fight or something?"

"No," I mumble.

Bianca's still standing there, not helping with the calves and looking totally confused. I haul the smallest calf in the corner up to her feet and start leading her toward an open teat. Bianca's still staring at me, wanting the goods, so after an irritated huff, I blurt, "We kissed, okay? A couple of times."

And confusion turns to outright joy. Bianca's face lights like a freaking Christmas tree.

"Stop it." I point at her.

"Stop what? This is awesome! Hayden is such a great guy! I'm so glad he's—"

I raise my hand to shut her up. "Ever since we've crossed that line, it's just been weird. Our first date was a total disaster." I focus on the calves and fair feeding while I describe the date in all its embarrassing detail.

Bianca's laughing so hard by the end, she actually has to wipe tears from the corners of her eyes. "Oh, that's bad. Poor Hayden."

"You can stop laughing now!" I snap, then shake my head with a sigh. "I don't know, Bee. Maybe we shouldn't have crossed that line. We were better off as friends. There's all this pressure now, and it's like we've forgotten how to just be together."

Bianca swallows down the last of her giggles, looking concerned over what I just said. "You've got to be kidding. Hayden's awesome. I bet he's totally romantic. He'd be such a great boyfriend."

"Then you date him."

Bianca frowns. "I'm taken, and very happily so. Come on, what's wrong with Hayden? I'm sure these are just some early teething problems that can be worked through. I bet it's weird going from friends to lovers."

"Can you not call it that? We're not *lovers*."

Bianca giggles. "It's just an expression."

I shudder. An expression I really don't like. When Hayden ran his fingers down my arm yesterday, asking if we should go somewhere secret, it fully freaked me out. Does he want to take things to the next level already? I'm so not okay with that. I scratch my jacket, trying to get to the itchy spot on my forearm.

"Stace, what is it? You look like you're about to throw up."

"I just..." Tears suddenly start to burn. "Why did I kiss him? I don't know if I can be anyone's girlfriend right now. I don't know if I want to get physical... or do any of that romantic stuff."

Bianca's face morphs with sympathetic understanding. "The Jonas thing? That wasn't romantic. That was cheap and sleazy."

"You know what I mean." I flick my hand in the air, then start scratching the calf's back as its little tail slaps into my leg. "Not that Hayden would ever do something like that to me, but I still feel…" I tut and sniff, shaking my head. "How am I supposed to date someone when I've got that gnawing, horrible history in the back of my mind?"

"Sounds like you need to talk it through with someone."

I roll my eyes.

"I'm serious. I so did not want to go see the psychologist over this me not eating thing, but we've ended up talking about other stuff, getting to the root of my insecurities. And that's after only two sessions." She holds up two fingers, and I glare at them.

"I'm not going to see some psycho."

Bianca grins. "Psychologist. There's a big difference."

"You know what I mean!"

"Fine, then talk to someone else. Tell Hayden what's going on in your head. That might help with—"

"Are you crazy?" I flick my arms wide. "Tell him what Jonas did to me? Not in a million years!"

"Why not? He'd understand. He's the sweetest gu—"

"He would so *not* understand! How would you feel if

you knew people had seen Cam totally naked and having sex with another girl?"

This shuts Bianca up quick. She goes still, swallowing hard, like she's actually imagining Cam doing it with someone else.

I snap my fingers in front of her face. "Let's just drop this, okay? You're probably right about the teething problems thing. Hayden and I just need to figure out what the new us looks like."

I don't know how the hell we're supposed to do that when I can't even figure out what *I* look like at the moment.

Who am I right now?

I'm not the girl I was before my parents died. I'm not the girl I was with Jonas. But parts of the me from back then are still inside of me. Which ones do I cling to? Which ones do I let go?

I frown, trying to focus back on the calves and not stress about how lost I feel.

7

WILLOW

I t's still windy this morning, though not as bad as yesterday. There's a cold bite in the air, which whistles through my clothing as I dash into school. Wrapping my arms around myself, I weave through the crowd, looking for April. Hopefully she's in our usual spot, loitering outside homeroom.

Heath's kind of right.

She really is a goody-goody, always likes to be at class before the bell rings. She likes to please. She likes it when teachers praise her and tell her how impressed they are.

But there's nothing wrong with that, right?

I used to love it when my parents went on about how great I was.

I frown, trying not to think about how much I miss

them, trying instead to figure out why Heath is so critical of a sister who is mostly sweet and kind. I guess she gets a little snappy with him, but she's been awesome at helping us out.

Shit. I should have gone to see her yesterday, even just for half an hour.

I need to make sure I spend as much time with her at school as I possibly can. She's my friend, and I don't want to permanently damage what we've got going.

Turning the corner, I find her leaning against the wall outside our homeroom door. Her short bob is tucked behind her ears, kept in place by brown bobby pins that match her hair. Her round face, usually so meek and shy, is pulled into a sullen frown.

Oh boy. Here we go.

Pasting on a smile, I skip up to her with a friendly "Hey."

"Hi." April slides her phone into her bag, then looks to the floor like it's a painting in an art gallery. Something to be studied.

"I'm sorry yesterday didn't work out." For a second, I contemplate telling her the truth about Heath not wanting to share me, but I'm pretty sure that'll just piss her off. Biting my lips together, I scramble to make amends. "You know what? On Tuesday, let's go out.

Just you and me. I'll tell Heath ballet's canceled or something."

April raises her eyebrows. "You're gunna lie to your boyfriend now too?"

The snippy statement feels like a slap to the face. Dipping my head, I swallow and wonder how to recover.

"I wouldn't do that if I were you," April mutters. I glance up, taken aback by her serious expression. "Heath wouldn't like it."

I don't like the way she says that, like she's implying that Heath owns me or something. It's not like that. We love each other. I *want* to spend time with him.

I don't say that, of course. I'm trying to make things better. Instead, I shrug and try to sound braver than I feel. "Well, I'll just tell him that I need your help with something important."

"Like what?"

I wince. "Like the fact that Harper's figured out the ballet school isn't charging her for the extra lessons I'm taking. If I don't put some kind of fake invoice together, then she'll know I'm not actually taking any extra classes. I don't want her to call the school and get chatting to someone."

April's eyebrow arches. "Have they phoned her about

the fact that you keep skipping the one class you are supposed to be taking?"

"No. Thankfully. Hopefully they won't. I'm sure they don't care too much as long as they get paid."

"I wouldn't count on it. Someone's going to follow up at some point, surely."

"I've been calling in with excuses each time, so as long as I keep doing that, they should just buy into it. I've told them I'll probably quit at the end of the term, but I still need to keep these invoices coming in. Do you think you could help me put together a fake one?"

April frowns. "But if she starts paying the school more, that'll show in their records, and they'll definitely call about it."

Crap! I hadn't thought of that.

Chewing my lip, I gaze out the window, shifting sideways to let a group of girls walk past. An idea hits me just as their excited chatter moves past us. I click my fingers and point at April. "What if we change the bank account number?"

"Harper will notice that."

"Yeah, but we can put on the invoice *'please note change of details'* or something."

April tips her head, her eyebrows bunching together. "That could work, I guess."

"Yes!" I grin and reach for her arm, lightly squeezing it. "Please help me. You're so good with all this computer graphic-y stuff, and I'm screwed if I can't make this work." I pull the invoice out of my bag and show her. "Do you think you could recreate something like this?"

April looks at it with a reluctant sigh. "Can't you just tell your sister the truth?"

"That I've been skipping classes to secretly date an older guy? Uh, no. She would freak out."

April doesn't say anything, and I wish I could read her mind. Or maybe not. Her eyebrows are only getting closer together as she scowls at the invoice in her hand.

The bell rings and I jolt before putting on a bright, pleading smile. "So, will you help me?"

April glances at me, her frown turning sad. "Are you sure, Will? Are you sure you want to keep going with this?"

"With what?"

"The choices you're making." April opens the door, and I follow her into class with an irritated huff. Just because she doesn't like her brother…

"Hey, I love Heath. This is the only way I can see him." I go over a conversation we've had way too many times before.

April looks sad and slips into her chair, tucking the

invoice into her folder. I sit down next to her, feeling edgy and nervous. She still hasn't given me a clear answer on the helping me thing, and I have to convince her. I don't have anyone else I can go to about this.

I lean over and nudge April with my elbow. "So…?"

With a heavy sigh, she nods. "Yeah, okay. Meet me in the computer lab at lunchtime."

"Yay!" I give her a relieved hug. "You're the best!"

She pats my shoulder and pulls away, getting her computer out for the lesson.

I follow suit, buzzed that my problem has been solved.

April is so awesome.

I have to think of something cool to pay her back for her essential help.

Seriously, I owe her so much. She's my one and only friend at North Ridge High, and I'm in love with her brother. Without her, I'd have nothing.

8

STACEY

The lunch bell rings, and the class starts packing up their books while the teacher calls out various instructions.

"Assignments must be handed in by Friday at three o'clock. I want to mark them over the holidays, and I will not accept late entries. Be responsible, guys. Make me proud."

I grin at Mr. Shafer as I glide out the door, secretly triumphant that all I have left to do is proofread my essay before handing it in. I think this is one of the first times ever that I haven't had to pull an all-nighter.

I guess trying to avoid thinking about Hayden yesterday worked in my favor on that score.

But I can't avoid it now.

It's lunchtime.

He'll want to hang.

Just like he did at morning break. I mean, it wasn't too bad. We just sat there with Bianca and Missy, talking about schoolwork mostly. It was safe, and only a little boring. Exactly what I needed.

But lunch is like fifty minutes.

Fifty minutes.

And Hayden's already hinted that he'd love to have a little one-on-one chat with me.

Crap! I so don't want to.

What am I going to say to him? I don't want to hurt his feelings. I don't want to tell him the truth about Jonas. I can't exactly start voicing the chaos in my head, because I have no idea what will spew out.

I'd rather just—

"Stace!"

I spin around and see Luka running toward me. She's looking happy, and I laugh when she grabs my hand and lets out this excited squeal.

"What?"

"Oh my gosh, have you seen the new student teacher? He just started this morning."

"No." I grin at Luka's expression.

"He's so humunah-humunah-HOT!"

"Really? What subject?"

"PE." Her eyebrow arches with a *you know what I'm saying* kind of look, and I can't help laughing again. "The girls are going nuts. His name's Mr. Hamilton, but we've already dubbed him Mr. HellaYum."

I grin.

"You've got to come check him out."

Man, that's tempting. Not that I want to be drooling over a PE teacher or anything, but it'd be nice to know what all the fuss is about.

I'm just thinking of saying yes when Hayden approaches, ambling up with a sweet smile. "Hey, Luka."

"Hi, Hayden." She clears her throat, glancing at me sideways.

"Your hair's looking nice today."

"Thanks." She runs her hand down her ponytail and flashes me an awkward smile.

"How often do you condition?"

"About… three times a week."

"Nice." Hayden bobs. "That's probably why it's looking so good. Way too many people make the mistake of washing their hair every single day, and it just completely strips out the natural oils."

"Okay." Her eyes dart to mine, but I can't maintain contact, so I glance at Hayden, forcing a closed-mouth smile instead.

She obviously has no idea why I hang out with Hayden. And maybe that's why when he reaches out to touch my shoulder, I swivel out of the way before he can.

Hayden looks a little hurt by my sudden move, but I try to look oblivious to it, like I didn't know what he was going to do. We've had this talk. Why is he reaching out to touch me when we're trying to keep our relationship on the down-low?

"You coming to the music room for lunch?" His voice is so meek it's basically a whisper.

Luka's eyes bulge and she stares at the ground, obviously waiting for me.

What do I do?

Thing is, I'd much rather see what Mr. HellaYum looks like than have a serious discussion with Hayden about our relationship.

That's bad, I know, but I'm not ready to get all heavy with Hayden. I need some more time to process and figure out what I want to say to him.

"It'll only take a minute," Luka murmurs, her brown

eyes so hopeful.

I glance at Hayden, not wanting to hurt him, but needing to buy myself some time. "I'll meet you real soon. I just… Luka wants to show me something."

"Okay. Can I—?"

"It's a girl thing," I quickly interrupt him.

His expression crumples like he can tell I'm lying.

Crap!

"Let's go." Luka snatches my arm and starts pulling me away.

"I'll see you soon," I call over my shoulder, trying to appease him, but I don't think it really works.

I worry about it as we walk down the corridor, heading for the field. When I glance over my shoulder as we exit the building, Hayden has already gone.

Should I really be ditching him to go check out this new student teacher?

What is wrong with me?

Am I intentionally trying to sabotage our relationship?

We reach the courts and I stand on the sidelines, watching Melina and Kim messing around with a netball. This pang of longing tugs at my chest until Luka's pointing finger and excited little "There!" distracts me.

I follow her line of sight, and my mouth drops open just a little.

Holy crap.

He's freaking gorgeous.

Tall, muscly. He looks like Captain America without the neat hairdo. His hair is more of a messy spike, obviously styled that way. He has a broad, friendly smile, accentuated by a couple of days' worth of facial hair. It's that sexy, short stubble kind of look. He's playing a game of basketball with some Year 9 and 10 boys. I can tell by their uniforms and size. He's laughing while they chase him down the court, calling out encouragement when one of the smaller students manages to steal the ball off him.

"Oh, he's nice too. Look at him." Luka sighs, resting her head on my shoulder.

I let out an awkward laugh, struggling to take my eyes off him. Talk about a hottie.

Should I be feeling this way if I'm with Hayden?

I mean, he's gorgeous in his own way. He could be a catwalk model tomorrow if he wanted to be. He's got a beautiful face, and I love that about him.

So why can't I stop staring at Mr. Hamilton's muscly arms and body?

Oh my gosh, I am so confused.

I—

"Hey!" Melina shouts across the court. "You guys wanna play?"

She spins the netball in her hands, then launches it at me. I catch it, instantly loving the familiar feel of the ball between my fingers. Memories cascade over me, a smile tugging at my lips as I flash through all the hours of netball I played growing up.

I thought I'd hate playing without Mum in my life, but now that I'm holding the ball…

"Yeah, sure." The words pop out of my mouth before I can stop them and I shed my bag, jumping onto the court with a grin.

Luka trails after me, getting into the game as the four of us run around the court, playing two-on-two netball.

It's so much fun.

I forgot how good it feels to run and jump, catch and pivot.

I poise to shoot while Kim jumps in front of me, trying to block my shot. Flicking the ball up, I hit the rim, and it bounces off to the side.

With a chuckle, I chase after it, calling over my shoulder. "This is why I played wing attack and not goal shooter!"

Turning back around, I jolt to a stop when I find Mr. HellaYum standing there, his foot on the netball.

He grins at me, picking up the ball easily and resting it against his hip.

"That's some nice playing. You must have had a good season."

He points at the girls behind me.

"Oh no. I didn't play this year."

"Really?" His pale brown eyebrows jump high. "You're good."

"Yeah. Uh, thanks." I hold my hands out for the ball. "I just needed a year off."

"Maybe next year, then." He passes the ball back and winks at me.

I can't breathe for a moment. He's so freaking gorgeous.

When I turn and walk back to Luka and the girls, they're laughing at me, wiggling their eyebrows and making me blush.

"Oh, shut up."

I hurl the ball at Luka and get set to play another few rounds. I kind of like this energetic buzz traveling through my body right now. I forgot how much fun playing netball could be.

9

WILLOW

The hum of the computer lab is making me twitchy for some reason.

I gaze across the quiet space. There are only three of us in here. The guy down the end keeps running his fingers through his hair so it's standing up at funny angles. When he turns to look at me, it's an effort to fight my smile. He looks like a stressed-out version of those punk-rock monkeys at the zoo. What are they called again?

A cotton top tamarin.

That's it.

Classic.

I turn back to watch April as she twiddles on the computer, putting together a perfect-looking invoice.

She's not saying anything as she works, and the scowl on her face is making me squirm.

"You're doing so great. This looks perfect!"

April gives me a sideways glance, like she's insulted by my compliment.

I cross my arms and almost wish I hadn't asked her to do this for me, but it's not like I've got anyone else.

April and I became friends because we were the two loners. I watched her sitting by herself lunchtime after lunchtime, wondering if I should talk to her but not really knowing how to start a conversation.

Everything was so dead and gray back then.

But eventually she approached me. Just sat down beside me one day and started nibbling on her sushi. She offered me a little piece, and then she started talking about how annoying our French teacher was. It felt like the first time I'd smiled in like forever.

Life got better after that.

We had each other. Someone to talk to.

I don't want to lose that.

"What account number should I use?" April clips.

I blink at her question. "Uh, make one up?"

April shakes her head. "It won't go through if it's not legit."

"Do you have one I could use?" I wince and cross my fingers on my lap.

April's eyes bulge, and she looks at me like I'm crazy. "You want me to steal money off your sister?"

I hiss, realizing how bad that sounds.

"What if…" I chew my lip, my knee bobbing like crazy as I try to think of a solution. We're so close. "I know." I snap my fingers. "Why don't I tell her that I've secured a job… and it can pay the same as what she's giving ballet? That way, the money can go into your account, and then you can get it out for me and I'll just hand it back to Harper."

"She'll probably tell you to keep it, since you've *earned* the money." April uses very sarcastic air quotes when she says the word "earned."

I can't help a giggle. Her deadpan expression is funny. "A little pocket change isn't a completely bad thing."

"Willow," April snaps. "That's stealing."

"Shhh." I put my finger to my lips and glance over my shoulder, but the tamarin is hunched over the keyboard, not paying any attention. I turn back and whisper, "It'll be okay, and the whole job thing is perfect, because it gives me even more time. That way I can do ballet classes with Heath and my after-school job can be time spent with you."

"Thanks so much for fitting me in." April rolls her eyes.

"What is your problem?" I sit back with a frown. "Come on, April. I'm trying to make this work for everybody."

"By lying." She gives me a pointed look. "You're gunna get busted, and it'll all turn to shit. For what? My brother? He's not worth it."

The hairs on the back of my neck prickle. "He *is* worth it. And what's one more little lie? Don't you see how it will free me up even more?"

"This rabbit hole you're digging is only getting deeper and more complicated."

I huff and slam back into my chair, annoyed that she's not siding with me. What the hell does she know? Her parents are never around; she can do whatever the hell she wants. It's easy for her to sit here judging me when she doesn't have anyone she even has to lie to.

April's expression wrinkles, her shoulders sagging. "I'm just worried you'll get so lost in there that you'll never be able to find your way out."

"I don't want a way out. I love Heath."

"Does he love you?" She's so freaking skeptical, it pisses me off.

I lean forward and whisper-bark, "Of course he does! He tells me all the time."

April scoffs and mutters, "Words don't always mean much. You're proof of that."

Now the hairs on my arms are prickling too!

I'm so tempted to tell her to shove it, but I need that invoice, so I clench my jaw and grit out, "Have you put your account in yet?"

April's lips part, her expression kind of wounded. I glance away, not wanting to feel guilty over this. April doesn't understand because she's never been in love before. When you love someone, you do anything for them. Anything.

Pulling out her wallet with a sigh, April finds her bank account number and puts it in. The invoice looks so freaking legit.

I'm stoked and so relieved.

"Can you email me a copy and also print one?"

She does a few more clicks, and then I hear a swoosh. "It's done," she mutters. "You'll have to use your ID card to get the print copy. Just tap it on the dashboard and it'll take a credit from your school account."

"Thank you." I smile at her, but April just glares at me, shutting down the computer and stalking out of the room without another word.

10

HAYDEN

Well, this afternoon has been a total suck-fest. I need to speak to Stacey about how she ditched me at lunchtime. I waited there the entire time and she never showed.

With an irritated grunt, I shuffle past students, heading for the main parking area. Out of the corner of my eye, I spot Denny and Carlos—the two guys who harassed me without mercy for most of this year.

"You gunna cry, crybaby?"

Even the memory of their bullying makes me shudder.

My survival instincts go on alert, but they turn the other way like they don't see me. I can't help a little smirk. They've stopped hassling me since I went crazy psycho on them, using my school bag as a weapon and lashing out until they ran away. I thought I'd just scared them as a one-off, but my show of unexpected fight obviously put them off completely.

I'll take it.

I wish I'd known I could do that months ago, but I'd been on a mission to save Bianca and Cam's relationship. It was a worthy cause and gave me the courage I needed to stand up to those bullies.

If only I could find the same courage right now.

I need to talk to Stacey, but I don't really know what to say to her.

Do I come in strong, pissed off, demanding answers?

Or do I act like her no show was really no big deal?

But it was. Every second that ticked by without her arriving hurt more and more. I ended up hanging out alone in the music room because Missy and Bianca went to have lunch with Cam. I played the piano for a while, sang, fought a few tears, then ended up playing GardenScapes on my phone until the bell rang.

I left the room feeling completely sorry for myself, but now I'm kind of annoyed. I waited there like a complete sucker. That's not cool.

Huffing out a breath, I march out of the main building and scan the parking lot in time to see Tane pulling away. I'm pretty sure that's Stacey's blonde hair in the back seat.

Awesome.

She didn't even stick around after school to say goodbye or apologize.

If that's not making a statement, I don't know what is.

Rubbing the ache beneath my collarbone, I turn the opposite direction and start walking home. Pulling out my phone, I wonder if I should text Stacey. I've got some pretty fresh words bouncing around in my head right now.

But nah.

With a frown, I turn off my phone altogether and slip it into my pocket. I don't want to text her, hear from her or anyone right now. I just want to wallow.

My feet scuff the ground as I walk the two kilometers home. Dad won't let me drive the Mini to school on days that aren't raining. It's so stupid. I'm totally old enough now, but he doesn't want me slacking off on the exercise.

"Fine days you bike or walk. It's that simple, mate. You can drive on the weekend or rainy days."

I tried to argue but gave up pretty quick when Tom started laughing behind Dad's back. I get enough people snickering at me. I don't need my older brother to, as well.

The wind buffets my body as I trudge home. By the

time I walk in the door, my hair is a mess, and my shoulders are stiff and sore from hunching against the wind.

It's enough to cap off my foul mood, and I slam the door with gusto.

"Whoa." Shelley emerges from the master bedroom in a bathrobe with a towel wrapped around her head. She must have just gotten out of the shower. "You okay?"

"No." I throw my bag on the floor, knowing it's useless to lie to my sister-in-law. She's the closest thing I have to a mother now, and even though I don't like thinking of her that way, she's got this annoying trait of picking up vibes, just the way Mum used to.

"Wanna talk about it?"

"No."

"Okay. Um, how about I can tell you need to talk about it, so come into the bathroom and style my hair for me."

I trudge after her with no argument. She's probably right. I do need to talk, plus styling hair always makes me feel better about life.

She quickly towel-dries her hair, then sits down on the stool and hands me her brush. I unravel the cord around the hair dryer. Just grasping those two implements between my fingers makes me feel instantly better. I start brushing out her hair, the action calming me.

"Whenever you're ready." She looks at me in the mirror and winks.

"In a minute. Is this a date night or girls' night or what?"

"Date night."

"Fancy or casual?"

"Fancy. It's our anniversary."

"Really? Already?"

"Well, it's our *the night we first met* anniversary. Four years ago today."

"Oh, okay."

"I told Tom we have to do something nice because… well, because we haven't gone on a fancy date for ages."

I grin. "Where are you guys going?"

"I've already booked a table at Gothensburg for dinner, and then we'll stroll along the river before going to The Furnace for coffee and a late dessert."

"Oooo. Two restaurants in one night. Good move."

"I know, right? That's what your mum always used to make your dad do, just to stretch it out a little." She giggles. "I remember her telling me, 'That man would eat and run if I let him. He has no idea how to linger over food, and as for his romantic bone, I'm pretty sure it never developed.'"

I chuckle and shake my head. That's so true. Dad's a good guy, but a Don Quixote, he is not.

"She said Tom is just the same, but we'd never have to worry about you. 'He's the tender heart of the bunch. Whoever scores him will be one lucky lady.'"

The comment makes me freeze, my eyes starting to mist as I think about how wrong my mother was. I don't think Stacey feels very lucky right now. Why else would she ditch me, not text me, leave school without even trying to see me?

I clear my throat and study Shelley's hair for a moment, picturing a few different styles before settling on a 'do I saw in a magazine a few months ago. It was half up with these thin French braids, and the rest was kept down with luscious big curls.

I sniff and get to work, quickly drying her hair before starting with the intricate braiding.

Shelley holds bobby pins for me while I section her hair with my comb and start the delicate work.

"So… how long are you going to make me wait?" Shelley catches my eye in the mirror.

I sigh. "I really like Stacey. I told her so, and we kissed and I thought it was all good, but ever since we've stepped out of the friend zone, it's gotten awkward and weird."

Shelley gives me a sympathetic frown. "What do you think's made it weird?"

"I dunno!" I open a bobby pin with my teeth, then slide it into place, careful not to scrape Shelley's scalp. "Stacey's just kind of pulling away from me. She totally ditched me at lunch today. We were supposed to meet in the music room, and she never showed."

"No text or explanation?"

"Nada."

Shelley's manicured eyebrows dip together. "So, you think she's regretting the shift in your relationship?"

That question hurts like a punch to the stomach, but I can't start arguing because I think it's probably right.

Blinking at my burning eyes, I finish another braid and secure it.

"Well, you need to call her on it. If she's changed her mind, you have a right to know."

"I don't want to hear that she's changed her mind," I mutter.

"So you'd rather live with the torture of dating a girl who might not be into you?"

My chin starts to wobble and I sniff, rubbing my right eye before combing out another section of hair.

"I'm sorry, sweetie. I'm not trying to hurt you," Shelley says gently. "It's just not okay for her to say one thing and then act like she didn't mean it. That's not fair on you. She has to look you in the eye and be honest. And you need to do the same. Any relationship based on anything other than honesty is doomed to fail. Trust me on this. I've had experience. Before I met Tom, I was dating a two-faced dickhead. One of the things I love so much about your brother is that he is brutally honest. He's real. I never have to second-guess myself with him."

I nod, knowing firsthand that's the truth. Tom never holds back. Sometimes it stings, but at least you know where you stand. Mum was the same, although her approach was somewhat gentler.

Finishing up the last braid, I reach for the curling iron and get to work on the remaining hair. Shelley is going to look stunning. I wonder if she'll let me help her with her eye makeup. Stace and I watched a cool YouTube clip the other day, and I reckon I can make Shelley's eyes really pop. I'm about to suggest it when she eyeballs me in the mirror.

"Talk to Stacey at school tomorrow. You deserve the truth. And if it's bad, we'll deal with the aftermath. We're good at that, right?" She winks at me, and I'm reminded why I love her so much.

"Thanks, Shell." I give her a sad smile.

"Love you, kiddo."

We share a meaningful look in the mirror, and I'm suddenly overwhelmed by how grateful I am. Shelley's filled what we all thought would be a gaping hole after Mum died. I mean, the hole's still there, but Shelley definitely makes it feel a touch smaller.

11

STACEY

I sit in the back seat of the car, staring out the window. Bianca's humming in the front seat, then stops to chat to Tane about something that happened in the quad at lunchtime.

"No way. You're getting way better at passing the ball. We love having you in the circle," Tane assures her. "And then Tameka jumped in too. It's been great having some girls join, and that's all on you. You should be proud of yourself."

I don't hear Bianca's reply, because my mind drifts to the netball court and how much fun it was to pass the ball around between Melina, Kim and Luka. I should definitely do that again.

Man, I've come a long way, when I think about the fact that I never wanted to touch a netball again after Mum died. She was the one who coached me in China. She brought the sport to our international school. It was our thing, and I was damn good at it. Team captain and everything.

With Mum gone, I just couldn't stomach the idea of playing again.

But now…

Well, today was fun.

I only went to check out Mr. HellaYum but got so much more than I bargained for. It was awesome. Playing that way was—

"Oh shit!" I jolt upright, suddenly remembering the fact that I was supposed to meet up with Hayden after I'd gone with Luka.

I'll just be a minute. That's what I said to Hayden.

But I wasn't just a minute. I was the whole damn lunch, and I was so buzzed afterward that I didn't spare him another thought.

What the hell is wrong with me?

Is this yet another sign that we shouldn't be together?

I'm forgetting my boyfriend! My sweet, kind, lovely boyfriend. Who does that?

"What is it?" Tane glances into the rearview mirror.

My eyes bulge as I bite my lips together. Like I can

admit what I just did to Hayden. Bianca will be horrified. I'm so not in the mood for her reaction right now.

"Um." I scramble for an excuse, noticing the empty seat beside me. "We forgot Willow."

Tane laughs. "Nah, she's hanging out with April this afternoon. She caught up with me just as we were leaving."

"Oh. Cool." I slump back in my seat, relieved to have dodged at least that bullet. Bianca swivels around to look at me. I flash her a quick smile, then grab the phone out of my bag.

Pulling up my thread with Hayden, I quickly type:

I'm so sorry about lunch. I got caught up playing netball and...

Forgot.

I forgot you.

Can I seriously type that?

Deleting the text, I shove the phone back into my bag, wondering what the hell I'm supposed to do. I'll just have to see him at school in the morning. Hopefully by then I'll have a decent story to tell him. A truthful one, obviously, but I need to work on how I can make it sound like I didn't just completely forget about him.

That I'm not the worst girlfriend in the world.

Aw, man, is that what I should even be?

"So confused," I murmur under my breath. "So damn confusing."

12

WILLOW

I'm supposed to be hanging out with April right now —at least that's what Tane thinks. I couldn't exactly tell him that I needed to see my boyfriend after school because I'm upset and he's the only one who can make me feel better.

I'm out of breath by the time I reach the North Ridge Road Four Square, but as soon as I spot Heath sitting at a picnic table outside, I know it was worth it.

He's sitting with a couple of guys from work. They're all in shirts and ties, sipping iced coffees from plastic bottles while checking their phones and talking at the same time.

Huh, so Heath's phone is working, then. I tried to call him after school, but when it kept going to answer phone, I spent a few minutes Googling his company and rang the head office instead. The receptionist was very helpful when I pretended to be April and said I had an urgent message for him.

"Oh, his sister. How nice to finally talk to you."

"Thanks. Do you know where he is?"

"If he's not answering his phone, then he's probably with a client, but I can tell you that around three thirty most days, they stop at the North Ridge Four Square for a quick coffee break."

I nearly squealed with glee.

That was just down the road from school!

"Thank you so much." I hung up with a grin and started running.

Heath hasn't seen me yet, and I take a minute to catch my breath and smooth my hair back into its ponytail.

"Yeah, right. She was an easy one! Hung off every bloody word I said." The guy opposite starts laughing, and Heath and his friend join in.

Aw man, I love Heath's smile. It's wide and beautiful. He looks so carefree right now. It makes me pick up my pace again, and I'm soon standing by the table.

Conversation ceases to exist the second I approach. Heath's eyes bulge, his nostrils flaring slightly. I don't understand his expression. Shouldn't he be happy to see me? I'm his girlfriend!

The guys eye me up and down, obviously confused by why I'm standing there.

Heath sniffs and smooths down his tie before screwing the cap back onto his empty bottle.

My insides are writhing jelly as I lightly brush my fingers on the table near his hand. He flinches away from me, then casually flicks his thumb my way.

"This is my sister's friend, Willow," he mutters, like I'm this annoying rash he can't explain. *I don't know where it came from. It just appeared and I need to get rid of it.*

Forcing a smile, I raise my hand and wave at them. "Hi."

They nod, still looking kind of confused. One of them takes a long drag from his cigarette, eyeing me from my forehead to my toes as he blows a stream of smoke out of his mouth. "Nice uniform."

Heath scowls at him before turning his dark gaze on me. "So what do you want?" His voice is so terse. It stings. Why is he acting like this?

"I just…" I smooth a hand down my ponytail and look at the sun-warped tabletop. "Wanted to talk to you."

"About April? Yeah, all right. I've got a minute." He stands from the table, rolling his eyes like his sister and her friend are such a pain in the ass.

One of the guys snickers as Heath leads me around to

the back of the shop. We step through a small alley, and when we reach the back shop door next to the large green dumpster, Heath snatches my arm and spins me around.

"What are you doing here?" he snaps.

The look on his face kind of scares me and I blink for a second, struggling to speak, "I-I called your-your work and she said—"

"You what?"

I flinch again. His voice is so harsh right now, and his grip on my arm is starting to hurt me. I try to wriggle free, but his hold only intensifies.

"How are we supposed to keep this a secret if you start calling my work?"

"You didn't answer your phone, and I need—"

"You can't just show up in front of those guys out there. Leave a message and I'll call you back!"

"But I thought your friends were okay with us being together. I thought you'd be happy to see me."

"Those are different friends. These are my workmates. They don't know about you! And my boss sure as shit doesn't!"

"Okay. I'm sorry," I whisper, still trying to wriggle my arm free, but he won't let me go.

"You didn't tell my boss you're my girlfriend, did you?"

"No." My eyes well with tears. "I spoke to the receptionist. I pretended I was April and said I was looking for you. She told me you have coffee here sometimes." I sniff. "I needed to see you. April's pissed off with me, and—"

"I'm seeing you tomorrow, all right? We can talk about it then, but don't show up like this. You break the routine and we'll get busted."

I blink at my watery eyes, trying to stop the tears. Heath tuts, pulling me into a tight embrace. It's rough and suffocating, but it's better than the painful arm grip. I don't wrap my arms around his waist. I just lean against his chest, fighting my tears.

"People won't understand, Will. They won't understand how much we love each other. That's why we can't tell anyone. You know that." He yanks me away from him and lightly shakes me. "Tell me you won't do this again."

"I won't." The words pop out of me like they're afraid to do anything else.

Heath's expression instantly relaxes, replaced with the kind smile I first fell for. "That's my girl." He runs his fingers down my face. "Now stay here until I'm gone. Then you can come out."

"I need a ride home."

"You'll have to call someone. I've got work."

He walks away without another word, and I wrap my arms around my waist, pushing them into the hollow ache inside my stomach. I don't know why, but I suddenly feel like curling into a little ball and crying.

Heath disappears down the alley, and I stay where he told me to, lightly rubbing my arm, which still kind of hurts. He's a strong guy. I've always loved his strength, but maybe not when it's directed at me like that.

A noise to my left makes me jump. The back mesh door swings open, and Manu walks out with two bulging black rubbish bags. He's wearing a Four Square apron over his school uniform and looks about as happy to be here as I am.

I wrinkle my nose and keep rubbing my arm as Manu flicks up the lid of the dumpster and throws the bags inside. Stepping back off the upturned crate, he rubs his hands on the back of his pants and stares at me.

"Who was that?" He tips his chin toward the spot Heath just disappeared from. "That fulla you was talking to."

"No one." I swallow and look away from him, my nerves pinching painfully.

"Didn't look like no one."

Oh shit! He was watching? What did he hear?

I want to walk away, but Heath told me to stay put until he'd gone. I don't want to annoy him again. Clenching my jaw, I jiggle my legs, counting to one hundred and hoping that's enough time.

"Your arm okay?"

I drop my hand, tucking it behind my back as Manu slowly walks toward me. He stops right beside me, and I'm instantly aware of how tall he is. Not Cam tall, but he's probably just over Tane's height. He's long and wiry, no bulk like Heath or Cam. It's like the gods have stretched him out a little early and he still needs to grow into his height.

His amber eyes search my face and I roll my shoulders, the silent gaze disconcerting. I'm about to snap at him to piss off when he quietly says something that makes me cold.

"He shouldn't be shaking you like that."

My chin starts to tremble as my defenses clink together, quickly forming a spiky layer of prickles. Manu doesn't know Heath at all. What gives him the right to stand there making judgments and telling me what he should and shouldn't be doing!

"He your boyfriend?"

"It's none of your business," I whisper.

"He looks kinda old."

"It's none of your business."

"You're only fifteen still, ay?"

"It's none of your business!" My arms shoot out like cannons, pushing him in the chest until he stumbles back with surprise. "Stay out of this," I screech, surprised by my venom.

I glance down at my shaking hands and wonder why I feel like crying again. And what the hell possessed me to push him? I've never done that to anyone before. What is wrong with me?

Manu lightly rubs his chest, his expression kind of shocked and maybe a little wounded. "Just want to help. You's got to be careful of a fulla like that."

I suck in these shaky, uneven breaths.

Oh no!

Is our secret about to get exposed?

I need to shut Manu up! Get him away from me!

"The only *fulla* I need to be careful of is you, sticking your nose in where it doesn't belong." What is up with my voice right now? I barely recognize it. And why am I pointing at him like he's the accused?

I quickly drop my finger, tucking it behind my back.

Manu's dark eyebrows bunch in the middle, but not with anger. He looks more worried than anything.

Is that worse?

I don't know.

I spin away from him so I don't have to see it.

"Manu! Get back to work." We both glance at the irritated Indian man standing at the back door. "I don't pay you to stand around talking to girls. And you." He points at me. "The back of the shop is for staff only. You go!"

I stumble back from his pointing finger and edge toward the alley while Manu shuffles away to the door. He stops just before going inside, glancing over his shoulder once more to give me another wounded frown.

Stepping into the alley, I hide from view, leaning against the wall and counting again. My arm still hurts and I give it a light rub, but now my insides feel kind of sore too. I need to get out of here!

Listening for voices out the front, I don't hear much and am pretty sure the coast is clear. So I edge to the end of the short alley and peek my head out to find the picnic table empty.

I brush my hands over the rough wood and pull out my phone.

Who do I text for a ride?

The idea of getting into the car with any of my family doesn't sit right, so I end up calling a taxi, which takes forever to arrive and costs me nearly all my monthly allowance. But at least I can sit in the back and not have to talk to anybody.

As I trudge up the driveway, I realize I don't have words to explain my behavior this afternoon. I don't have words for any of this crappy day. Hopefully, when I get to the house, I can slip in the door and head to my room unnoticed, because the idea of trying to hold a normal conversation right now feels impossible.

13

HAYDEN

The wind whips a flurry of new spring blossoms off the tree. They fall about my feet, dancing a circle as I wait out the front of school for Stacey to show up.

I texted her last night to ask if we could talk before the first bell rang.

All I got back was a simple *Sure thing*.

No smiley faces or gifs. No emojis.

I'm not sure what's happening to us at the moment, but hopefully today's conversation will clear it up. Man, I'm nervous.

I've already rehearsed what I'm going to say a hundred times over. I just hope the words will stick. When you're lying awake in bed at night, it's easy to come up with the perfect speech, but sometimes it leaves you in the morning. Hopefully my constant repetition has cemented it.

The white—well, kind of brown— station wagon that's in desperate need of a wash pulls into the lot, and I wait by the tree, forcing myself to stay put. Bianca's the first out of the car. She shuts the door and races across the carpark to greet her boyfriend. Cam's got such a huge smile, and it only ever gets bigger when he sees her. Picking her up, he gives her a morning hug and kiss. She laughs at something he said, and for just a second, I wish I was him. Tall and broad and strong.

I could probably lift Stacey like that if I really wanted to, but it's not like I could hold her for long. Curse my stupid, weakling arms.

"Hey." Stacey approaches, tucking her thumb under her bag strap and giving me an uneasy smile.

"Hi." My voice squeaks and I quickly clear my throat, then tip my head to the right. "Let's go this way."

"Okay." Stacey bobs her head and follows me around the corner. I don't stop walking until we reach the big gymnasium. It's kind of cold, but there's no one around, and I want to have a private conversation.

Stacey shivers and wraps her jacket a little tighter around her neck. The wind whips her long fringe across her face. She tucks it back and gives me a sad smile.

"I'm sorry about lunch yesterday. I got caught up playing netball with the girls."

"Netball." I raise my eyebrows. I thought she never wanted to do that again.

"Yeah. It was actually really fun." She looks confused for a second, but then starts to smile like she's reliving a delicious memory.

I'm about to smile with her and tell her how great that is when her eyes suddenly bulge and she dips her head.

With a confused frown, I glance over my shoulder and spot a gorgeous guy strolling toward us. He's young, but obviously not a school student anymore.

"Hey. How's it going?" He grins at both of us, but his eyes linger on Stacey.

She smiles at him and quietly croaks, "Hi."

He strolls past, and I don't say anything until he's all the way around the side of the building. "Who's that?"

"New student teacher." Stacey clears her throat, brushing a finger across her red cheek.

Great. She's freaking blushing.

"Mr. Helim or Hamil or something like that."

I study her flustered expression and my stomach pitches. Oh yeah. I know why she got distracted with netball yesterday. He was probably on the courts too.

Being the cool student teacher who hangs out with the kids at lunch. Playing a little ball with his cool smile and big muscles.

I can't help a little scoff as I shake my head. Screw the speech. I may as well just say it like it is. "I get it."

"Get what?" Stacey's forehead wrinkles.

"I'm not your type, right? You thought for a second that maybe I was, because we get on so great. But then you kiss me and it all gets real and you suddenly realize that I'm just… not manly enough." I throw my arms wide. "I'm not a bloke with ripped muscles. I'm not a PE teacher in butt-hugging shorts with metallic thighs and a Colgate smile. No, I want to be a hairdresser and I find fashion interesting, which obviously makes me gay, right? Because gay guys aren't allowed to be manly, and heterosexuals aren't allowed to be whatever the hell I am."

Her lips part, but no sound comes out.

"You're embarrassed by me, aren't you? You can't stomach the thought of dating someone who can't lift you off the ground or look all cool and sexy beside you. You don't want to be my girlfriend because you're worried people might laugh behind our backs. 'Why's Stacey dating *him*?'"

Her eyes round and her breathing's gone funny.

"Feel free to stop me at any point with a 'No, Hayden, that's not it.'"

Her expression crumples, and she looks to the ground.

Great. She's not even freaking denying my rant!

I huff and look away from her, shaking my head. "You know what? Screw you, Stace. If you don't want to kiss me in public, then don't kiss me at all! Don't be my girlfriend, okay? I don't need some sympathy crush."

I stalk off, my heart racing and breaking at the same time. I can't believe I just did that. I've wanted her for so long, pined for her. Then I finally start dating her, for all of two seconds, before laying out an emotional rant and basically dumping her!

I'm such an idiot!

As I storm into the building and out of the cold, it suddenly dawns on me what I've just done. The words spewing out of my mouth come back to me in fragments, joining together like this ugly jigsaw puzzle.

"Oh shit," I whisper and am about to spin back and run after Stacey when I'm stopped by Bianca.

"Are you okay?" She touches my arm while I suck in a breath and nearly burst into tears.

Seriously? I'm gunna cry now too?

"What happened?" Bianca's looking really worried.

I slump my shoulders and sniff. "I think I just dumped Stacey."

"What?" Bianca's green eyes bulge, her pale, freckled face morphing with sympathy.

"Oh, this is all such a mess." I start fanning myself. A couple of girls walk past, snickering into their binders. I don't care. I'm all hot and prickly. My breaths are getting punchy.

"Come on." Bianca snatches my wrist and pulls me toward the music rooms, hauling me into the first practice room that's free. As soon as the lights are on and the door is closed, she spins on me with the one question I don't want to answer. "Why would you dump Stacey?"

I start pacing the small space, unzipping my jacket and accidentally knocking my knee on the bass drum. I give it a rub while Bianca reveals just how much she knows.

"You only just got together."

Stacey must have told her. Great. I wonder what she said to her twin.

"I'm dating Hayden, but I'm really not sure. He's such a girl. Please don't tell anyone. It's so embarrassing."

My guts are writhing. I bend over and slump down on the stool. "I know, but she's been acting weird and, like, pulling away. I tried to call her on it, and when I did, she didn't say anything. Didn't deny any of my claims, so I got shitty and told her to either kiss me in public or not at all."

Bianca cringes.

"Oh, stop it! I feel bad enough as it is. I just wish she'd said something, but she didn't! She just stood there, and instead of calmly trying to explain myself, I got all emotional and started spewing out this… this stuff! "

Bianca bites her lips together and tucks her skirt beneath her legs as she eases onto the spare seat beside the drum kit. "You know, Stacey has been through a bit of a rough time."

"What, with your parents?"

"Well, yeah, but also Jonas."

I wince. "Yeah, I know he screwed her and then dumped her. Asshole. And then I guess that whole porn thing really threw her as well."

"You know about that?" Bianca's eyes bulge.

"I just heard this rumor that Jonas was trying to start up some kind of porn site. It must have really hurt Stacey to know she was dating such a sleazeball."

"Yeah." Bianca's studying me like she's waiting for more.

"What?" I sniff.

"You didn't hear that rumor from Stacey?"

"No, all she's told me is that he dumped her and it was harsh."

"Yeah." Bianca swallows and averts her gaze. "Yeah, so her heart is still kind of fragile, and maybe she doesn't want to go public because she's afraid of having a repeat or—"

"But I never would. I'd only ever treat her with respect and care. I'd never intentionally hurt her. I really care about her." Bianca smiles as I deflate. "I really care about her, and I just treated her like shit. I just hurt her!" I cover my face with my hand and wail.

Bianca lightly shakes my arm "Hey, it's okay. You're not the only one to blame. She should have engaged in the conversation too. We just need to find out why she didn't. Don't worry. We can fix this."

"How? She probably never wants to see me again."

"Let's just give her a little breathing room today. I'll check in with her and try to get a gauge on how she's feeling. What we need is for you guys to just spend a little quality time together, outside of school, away from rumors and prying eyes. Just a chance for you guys to really talk it through. Maybe you could..." She gasps and snaps her fingers. "The camping trip! We're going away with Beck, and we're each allowed to bring a friend. It'll be like this intimate, safe group of people who all care about each other. You could take her for a long walk in the forest, and it'd be the perfect place to figure it all out. No cell phone coverage. Complete isolation in the bush. And you could also test out being a couple in front of us. If it goes well, I'm sure Stacey will feel more confident about dating you at school. Do you know what I mean?"

I lower my hands and look at her hopeful expression. "Yeah. I guess so, but… are you sure she'd want me there?"

"*I* want you there. You're my friend too, right?"

"Of course I am, but what about Cam?"

"Tane can invite him." Bianca shrugs like this is the easiest solution in the world.

It would probably be a good chance to get Stacey on her own for a while. We could stroll along a track, holding hands and chatting. At this time of year, none of the forests will be very busy. Bianca's right. It'd be a great opportunity to really hash this out. My lips twitch with a nervous smile. "Are you sure about this?"

"Yes! Trust me. My sister and you are great together. You just need a chance to figure out what that really looks like. This weekend away will be the perfect chance." I can't help an excited little squeak. Bianca laughs and pulls me into a hug. "You're the best, Hayden. I want my sister with someone as awesome as you. We just need to help her see past her… well, her past."

I chuckle and give Bianca a little squeeze, so relieved she's my friend. That she's on my side. Our side. Stacey and me. We are a good fit. I used to be one hundred percent convinced of that, and I don't want to give up on that dream. Not just yet. This weekend, I'm going to win back my girl, and I won't screw it up with stupid, thoughtless, emotional rants.

14

WILLOW

Something's been bugging me ever since I left the Four Square, and I didn't figure out what it was until I woke up at 2:00 a.m. When I first got home, Harper and Ozzy were down at the milking shed. Bianca, Cam and Stacey were cooking dinner, and I took my chance to sneak upstairs and try to get my shakes under control.

I've been shaking.

I don't know why, but my body can't sit still.

When I dragged my sleep-deprived butt out of bed this morning, I actually had a coffee, hoping it'd help to equalize me. But I don't normally drink coffee, and now my shakes are even worse. I've been doing my best to hide them by sitting in the back seat on the way to school and clamping my hands under my legs.

But I think the only thing that's really going to work is talking to Manu.

See, it occurred to me as I lay in bed listening to Harper's breathing and trying not to get freaked out by the different shadows in the room that Manu could totally ruin my life. If he says anything to Tane about the *fulla* behind the Four Square, I'm screwed. Tane's not the type of guy to shrug something off. He's a protective "cousin," and that's a dangerous thing for me right now.

There's no way around it. I need to track Manu down this morning and make him promise not to say anything to anyone.

I've had a few freak-out moments since the revelation that Manu's already called or texted Tane, but thankfully my "cousin" hasn't approached me and quipped, "So I hear you're dating a guy we've never heard of. I hear he's not in high school anymore. Want to explain that to me?"

He'd never understand. Harper would freak out and make Beck tell me to never leave the house again.

That's not happening.

Heath and I know people don't get it. That's why we have to protect our relationship. That's why I shouldn't have surprised him yesterday. I've already texted to apologize. He's forgiven me and told me how much he's looking forward to seeing me this afternoon.

See, I thought *that* being resolved would make me feel better, but it didn't. Because it's actually the whole Manu thing that's been eating at me. I have to sort it out before I see Heath or he might get annoyed again, and I don't want our precious ballet minutes to be ruined with an argument.

I hurry down the school corridor, searching for Manu as I go. What's the bet he's late. He's always late. People laugh and call it Moo Time, but it's freaking annoying. My parents were sticklers for time. They said if you arrive late, you're showing disrespect to the person waiting for you.

"Why is your time more valuable than theirs?"

Mum's voice echoes in my head, and I tense my shoulders, not wanting to think about her. Not wanting to wonder what she'd think about me dating Heath.

Snapping my eyes shut for just a second, I try to shake her from my head and end up breaking into a slow jog, weaving around students until I finally spot Manu near the Year 12 lockers. I'm glad I returned here to check. The bell's about to ring any minute, but I need to do this now. Even if it means being just a little late to class.

"Psst!" I try to get his attention as I glide past.

He glances at me with a frown and I tip my head. His frown only deepens, so I bulge my eyes at him, irritated that he's not picking up my *follow me* message more quickly.

His forehead is fully wrinkled now, and I roll my eyes, tipping my head with extra exaggeration until his dumb ass finally picks up the cue.

Mumbling something to the guys he's standing with, he hitches his bag onto his shoulder and follows me. I stay a few paces ahead of him, hoping people won't look at us and think we're together.

Leading him away from the crowded locker areas, I weave down a couple of corridors until I reach some steps and then race down and around the corner.

"Not supposed to be down here." Manu gives me a reproving look when he catches up to me.

"It's only for a minute," I snap. "I need to talk to you without the whole world hearing."

"What about?"

I clear my throat, licking my dry lips as my index finger picks up a steady beat against my elbow. "I need you to not tell Tane what you saw yesterday… behind the Four Square."

He doesn't say anything, his black eyebrows bunching together.

I have this sudden panic that he's already said something. Did he seek out Tane the second he walked into school, and that's why I couldn't find him straight away?

I gape at him, my voice shaking when I whisper, "You haven't said anything, have you?"

"Not yet."

"Thank God." I close my eyes, tipping my head back. "Please don't. It's not his business."

Manu goes quiet again and I look at his face, biting the inside of my cheek as I try to figure out what he's thinking.

"Moo? Can you promise me?"

He tuts, his face bunching with a frown. "Who was that guy?"

I swallow, wondering if I should downplay it. But even Manu's not that stupid. "He's my—" I lick my lips again. "He's my boyfriend, okay?"

"How old is he?"

"Twenty. And I know that that seems old, but in like three years' time, the age gap will be totally insignificant."

"You're fifteen, aren't you?"

"I turn sixteen in the school holidays."

He studies me for a long, painful beat. "You having sex?"

I bulge my eyes, heat flashing through me. "That is none of your business."

"I'm pretty sure that's illegal."

"What? No it's not!"

"Google it. Girls under sixteen shouldn't be doing it with an older fulla. No one under sixteen should be doing it at all. That's the law."

"How the hell would you know that?" I'm snapping again. And why is my heart suddenly thumping in my head?

"I heard it once, thought it was BS, so I looked it up. Sure enough. No sex 'til you're sixteen."

I clench my trembling jaw and sniff, still not willing to one hundred percent believe him. With a thick swallow, I get out of this embarrassing conversation with a little lie. "Well, we're not having sex, so… no law breaking."

Manu goes quiet again, like he doesn't believe me.

Who the hell does he think he is?

Standing there quietly judging me when he's probably been having sex for years. Manu can't help but get himself in trouble. I've heard Tane and Cam worrying about him before. He's a sloppy, reckless student who's made permanent butt marks in the chair at the principal's office.

I'm not going to trust a word he says, and I'm about to tell him so.

But I need him on my side.

Dammit.

Squeezing my eyes shut, I force a breath through my nose and soften my voice. "Look, I just… None of my family will understand. All they'll see is me dating an older guy, and they won't focus on the fact that we love each other."

"He loves you?"

"Yes." Why do people always sound so cynical when they ask that question?

"He shouldn't be hurting your arm and shaking you, then."

"He doesn't."

"He did yesterday. Has he ever hit you?"

"No!" I'm horrified by the suggestion. Heath would never do that. He loves me. "Yesterday was just…" I huff. "I'm fine and he loves me, so you don't have to worry about it." My voice is suddenly terse again, and I take another calming breath before practically pleading, "Please, Manu, I need your help. Just… keep this quiet. Please."

He sighs, looking down the corridor, his jaw muscles tensing over and over.

"Please," I whisper again, obviously sounding as desperate as I feel, because he glances down at me and nods.

"Okay, fine."

"Thank you," I breathe, relief flooding me.

"But he better treat you good, or I'm telling."

My body pings tight, and I frown at him. "You won't need to. He *loves* me."

"Yeah, you keep saying that."

I don't like the skeptical look on his face as he wanders away from me. It's kind of insulting.

But what do I care what he thinks?

I pull back my shoulders as the bell rings loudly above my head. I jump with fright, then close my eyes and huff.

I *don't* care what Manu thinks. Heath *does* love me.

Rushing up to class, I slip into homeroom and pull out my laptop while the teacher takes the roll. Something Manu said is bugging me, and it'll probably eat away until I freaking Google it.

My forehead wrinkles as I pull up a fresh window on Safari. With trembling fingers, I type in:

How old do you have to be to legally have sex?

A big **16 or older** pops up on the screen, and I quickly

exit the window. I don't want to read the blurb underneath. I'm basically sixteen. I mean, who has ever even heard of that law or bothers looking it up anyway?

Manu's weird.

Heath is awesome.

I'm cold. I don't know why.

Hunching down in my seat, I pull my jacket a little tighter around my body, reminding myself that disaster has been diverted. Manu won't tell and he'll never need to, because Heath loves me and will treat me good.

15

STACEY

I chew my gum, the minty flavor starting to lose its impact as I work my jaw up and down. Rereading the paragraph I just wrote, I frown and rub my eyes. I'll need to take out my contacts soon. They're starting to burn.

But I want to get this assignment done.

And Willow's in the shower anyway. I heard it flick on a few minutes ago, so the bathroom won't be free for at least five minutes. I scoff. There's no way I'll ever come to terms with that whole three-to-five-minute shower rule Beck insists on. With all the rain we've had over winter, you'd think he'd lighten up a little, but no, we have to think in advance. If we get another dry summer, we need the tanks to be full.

Blah blah.

With a huff, I squint my eyes and reread, for the third time, the lame introduction to my sociology essay.

I'm finding it so hard to concentrate tonight. Shuffling on my pillows, I adjust the laptop on my knee and glance down at my notes from today's lesson. But they barely make any sense. I was scribbling what the teacher said while thinking about... Hayden.

Dammit.

I didn't see him for the rest of the day. I actually purposely avoided all the places I know he likes to hang out. I can't decide how to feel about what he said to me —guilt, sadness, anger, indignation. It's impossible to settle, because maybe I'm feeling all of those things.

I should have told him that he was talking out his ass, that being unsure about him and me has nothing to do with the fact that I once thought he was gay. I mean, I don't think that's the reason. I love Hayden's flair and that we have so much in common.

So why didn't I say that?

Why didn't I slap my hand over his mouth, look him in the eye and tell him that he doesn't need to be some big, tough man for me to want him?

I go still, wondering why I'm struggling to answer that question in the privacy of my own bedroom.

Is that it?

Is Hayden right?

But I—

Wincing, I rub my forehead and wish this whole thing would just go away. After the whole Jonas affair, I thought I was over needing some deep physical attraction. I mean, Hayden's cute. His face is pretty. I love his eyes. He's a great kisser. So, what the hell is my problem?

Hayden is fun to be around. As much as I loved playing netball yesterday, I missed the music room today. I didn't want to be on the courts where my gaze would no doubt travel to the student teacher, so I sat in the quad with Tane and his mates, quietly nibbling my sandwiches while I listened to Tameka, Luka and Kim laughing over some TV show I apparently *have* to watch.

Bianca waltzes into the room, humming dreamily as she grabs her school bag and starts looking for something. I glare at her, knowing she's probably just spent the last few minutes making out with Cam or something.

"What?" She goes still, her cheeks flushing.

"Just don't," I mutter. "I'm glad you're happy. I'm glad you know exactly what you want, and that Cam is perfect, and you guys are totally in tune and like the ultimate couple goal."

Bianca's shoulders drop and she perches on the edge of

my bed. "I'm sorry about what happened with Hayden today."

"I don't want to talk about it. I don't want to talk about him or *any* guy." I fix my eyes back on my computer screen and the fuzzy black letters.

Bianca stays where she is, and the gum in my mouth turns stale when I glance up and catch the look on her face.

Now it's my turn to say, "What?"

"I, um. Well… I had a chat with him today."

My stomach pitches. "And?"

"He feels kind of bad about what happened and…" She purses her lips.

I wait with bated breath, but she just keeps sitting there until I slap my bed in frustration. "Bianca! Don't do that *leave me hanging* thing. It drives me crazy! *Finish* your sentences!"

Her nose wrinkles, and she quickly shifts to her bed.

Oh crap. She's created physical distance, which can only mean one thing.

She's done something I won't like.

With an irritated huff, I scowl at her. "What did you do?"

She winces. "I invited Hayden to come camping with us this weekend."

"What? Are you crazy?"

"No. He's my friend, and I want him to come."

"Bullshit!" I slap my computer closed. "After the way he spoke to me today, you're expecting us to just skip off on some camping trip and what? What do you think is going to happen?"

"Hey, you stayed silent, okay? Give him a break. He deserved some kind of response from you, and maybe if you'd just said something, he wouldn't have gone off on you."

I swallow and look away from my sister. Guilt hurts. It's scratchy. I don't like it.

"Look, he was really upset about this morning, okay? He wants to make it right."

"Oh really? His radio silence indicates otherwise." Okay, so that's new. I didn't realize that was bugging me as well, but when I think about it, I've been incessantly checking my phone since school got out.

I glare at the device on my nightstand, hating how black and inactive the screen is.

"Have you texted him?" Bianca drills me with a pointed look.

I work my jaw to the side, refusing to answer the question.

"He probably doesn't know what to say to you. He's hurt and embarrassed. Stacey, why didn't you tell him he was wrong when he was spouting off all that stuff?"

My shoulders slump forward, and suddenly I can't look at my sister, like at all.

"Are you... Do you seriously not like him anymore?"

"Of course I like him. He's a sweetheart and he's funny, but..."

"But what?"

I wrinkle my nose. How do I explain something I don't even understand myself? Bianca and I have already discussed the Jonas thing, and she thinks I should tell Hayden every detail.

Like hell.

So what do I say now?

That I find Mr. Hamilton attractive and I feel awful about it? That I don't know if I'll ever be able to go public with Hayden? That all these little signs keep piling on top of each other, telling me loud and clear that we were better off as friends?

I should probably just stick with Hayden's stupid assumption, because it's an easy out.

"Stace?"

"Hayden's not very… He's…" I sigh. "People think he's such a girl sometimes, and it can be embarrassing. And it's not like I'm lusting after him. I've never really felt that total zing when I look at him, you know? That physical pull? He's pretty, but he's not… well, you know. So maybe we *are* just meant to be friends."

Bianca's reprimanding look makes me feel small and irritated. "You must have felt something if you kissed him."

I purse my lips, trying to remember why I did kiss him that first time. And then the next day when he wanted to analyze the kiss, and it was just so adorable that I told him I liked him, and we kissed again and it was lovely and—

"So you're not letting yourself fall for this guy because he doesn't fit into your ideal mold? No one's perfect, Stace, and if that's what you're looking for, you're gunna be single for the rest of your life."

I flop back with a huff, wondering if that's such a bad thing, but then knowing myself enough to realize that I'm not the type who likes to be single. No matter how many scars Jonas left behind, I still want love again.

"Stacey, come on. Hayden is awesome, and sure, he might not be the strong guy who can literally sweep you off your feet, but—"

"It's easy for you to talk like this. You have a tall, strong guy who *can* sweep you off your feet."

"But he's not perfect," Bianca murmurs. "I mean, I feel bad saying that, because he's amazing, but he sucks at telling me how he feels about stuff. He spent months hiding the truth about his family from me, and that caused issues for us. Hayden has all the words, and they're sweet and kind and funny. You never have to worry about where you stand with him. He's honest and real."

I swallow, knowing she's right but struggling to admit it.

"Stacey, I know you don't want to hear this, but you had tall and strong. You had the guy you thought was so smoking hot, and look at what he did to you. Can you honestly look me in the eye and tell me you think Hayden would ever treat you that badly?"

My skin's getting all hot and itchy. I don't like it.

Scratching my neck, I keep my eyes on the ceiling and don't say anything.

"He may be different, but Hayden's a boyfriend you can trust. One you should be proud to have fall for you. So, he's coming camping with us. That'll give you the weekend to figure out how you really feel about him. If you can be a couple in front of the family, then I'm sure you can be a couple out in the big wide world as well."

I'm still not saying anything. Where's my voice gone? My snappy replies? I miss them.

"Please don't blow this, Stace," Bianca whispers. "Hayden's good. He's kind. He's—"

With a sharp huff, I get off the bed and leave the room. I need a chance to think, and I can't do that with Bianca harping on about how wonderful Hayden is. I know he's wonderful, all right? But what about physical attraction? That's important too.

You do find him attractive. He's beautiful, remember?

I growl in my throat and stomp down the stairs, only to stumble into another conversation I don't want to hear.

"So, I was wondering if it'd be okay to invite him on the camping trip?" Cam asks Tane.

"Who?" I blurt.

They both look at me, no doubt wondering why I'm scowling, but people just need to stop springing extra guests on me. This camping trip is going to be bad enough as it is.

Cam gives me a knowing smile, like Bianca's told him everything about me and Hayden. I glare at him and he raises his eyebrows, looking out the kitchen window and rubbing the back of his neck.

The kettle pops, and Tane answers my question while Cam dives for something to do.

"Manu. Something was bugging him at lunchtime today. He didn't want to tell us anything, but we figured the camping trip might perk him up a bit."

"I told him about it already," Cam says, glancing over his shoulder while he pours boiling water into the mugs. "He seemed interested. Wanted to know if everyone was bringing a friend." Cam hands Tane a mug and then smiles as Bianca steps into the kitchen. He passes her a milo, running his hand down her back before calling into the lounge, "Anyone else want a drink?"

"Nah, I'm good, mate. Thanks," Beck says from the couch, and Harper shakes her head. I do the same but stay in the kitchen when everyone else moves out of it.

"Willow's bringing a friend, right?" Cam pulls a chair out for Bianca, then takes the seat next to her at the dining room table.

Tane nods. "Yeah, I think so. I'm assuming that April chick."

"Manu was just checking. I think he doesn't want to crash our party if he's the only extra coming."

"Tell him he's welcome." Beck glances up from his book with a jovial smile. "He might be an idiot sometimes, but he's a good kid. I want to give him a second chance."

My upper lip curls, and I fight to put it back in place. I

can't exactly say anything. Manu's not a bad person. He did pay to watch me have sex with Jonas, but as soon as he realized it was me in the video, he stopped. Then he stepped up and got in major trouble to support me. I owe the guy, but I still hate that he's seen me naked.

Beck's obviously forgiven him.

And now he's coming camping with us.

Oh joy!

This weekend is just getting better and better.

16

WILLOW

I gaze at my phone screen, nervously biting the inside of my cheek while I wait for April to respond to my text. It's Wednesday. I have no ballet. I'm supposed to be up here in my room doing homework, but I can't concentrate.

April basically didn't speak to me yesterday or today. It's turning into a very lonely week at North Ridge High, and I can't stand it.

So, I'm holding out an olive branch.

Me: Harper bought the invoice. Didn't even question the account change. Woohoo! Freedom! Thanks for your help. Now I just need to think up a job I can do after school. Then you and me can have some hang time. Sweet! So excited for it.

April makes me wait like a whole three minutes for a

reply. I nearly give up and throw my phone onto the bed when finally she responds.

April: Good for you. Go forth and fabricate.

I frown at the message, irritated by her sarcastic reply.

Me: You don't have to be so mean about it. I'm freaking thanking you.

April: I don't want your thanks. I wish I hadn't helped you.

Me: What? So are you just gunna keep the money, then? Fine!

April: Of course I'm not going to keep your dirty money.

Me: You're not going to tell, are you?

April makes me wait again, and the inside of my cheek is starting to hurt.

April: No, I'm pretty sure Heath would kill me if I did.

That rocky feeling comes back into my gut. I scratch my upper lip and reply, trying to take the higher ground and end things on a good note.

Me: Well, thanks for understanding about us. You're the only one who does.

April: Don't fool yourself. I don't. I just feel like I'm caught in this thing, and I don't know how to get out of it without pissing off my bro. At first I was doing this to help you, because you're the only real friend I've ever had at North Ridge. But I don't feel like we're friends anymore. I feel like you're just using me so you can have your secret relationship.

Her words hurt, and I drop my phone, not wanting to deal with them.

My heart is thundering. My stomach is tight and uncomfortable. Snatching my phone, I send Heath an SOS. That's the only thing that will make me feel better. I need to see him. I *need* to.

Within moments, he texts back that he's coming, and I grab my stuff, racing downstairs so I can wait for him at the end of the driveway.

"Where are you going?" Harper stops me when I fling the front door open.

"Out. With April." I paste on a smile.

"You're supposed to be helping me with dinner." She frowns. "I was just about to call you down."

"Aw, please? April's invited me to her place for dinner." I put on my best puppy eyes, the lies rolling off my tongue so easily. Harper rolls her eyes and tries to go for a reprimanding frown, but I just bat my eyelashes until she chuckles.

"Okay, fine, you little squirt. Do you need someone to drop you?"

"No, April's dad is picking me up."

"I'd like to meet him." She starts drying her hands on a

tea towel, and my heart catapults into my throat when she says, "Should I come down?"

"No!" I give her a horrified glare. "How embarrassing is that? I'm not a baby. Don't you dare come out of this house."

"But—"

"No! Please, Harp. Don't treat me like this. I'm nearly sixteen."

Harper's obviously a little perplexed by my behavior, so I force a smile and try to explain myself in a way that she'll love.

"I'm sorry. I'm not trying to be difficult. I'm just finding my way, and the counselor told me that part of that is learning to do things on my own. I don't want you to mother me or baby me. And if I don't want that, then I have to start acting like an adult."

The counselor hasn't said anything like that to me, but Harper will never know. Thank God for patient confidentiality!

My older sister swallows and gives me a resigned smile. "Okay. But I would love to meet your friends at some point. April's coming camping, right?"

"Yeah. Hope so." I force a smile and duck out the door.

Stupid camping. I totally forgot about that.

I don't want to go!

I could try using ballet as an excuse, but I doubt they'll let me stay home for that. I could try staying with April, but I'm not sure she'll let me now that she's all pissy. This camping trip *is* really important to Beck. I really should go. I'll just have to make up an excuse for why April had to bail last minute.

Heath's just pulling up to the driveway when I reach the end.

I jump into his car, wrinkling my nose at the weird smell. It's like that dog poo smoke from the party, and I can't figure out what it is.

"Hey, sexy." He smirks.

As soon as we're out of sight of the house, he puts his hand behind my neck and pulls me over for a searing-hot kiss. He's still driving, and logically I know this is so super dangerous, but there's a heady rush to it as well.

I brush my tongue against his before he sucks my lower lip. He tastes like beer and cigarettes and—

A car beeps and he swerves, laughing as he pulls the wheel back into line and we race to one of our favorite make-out spots.

"So, what's the big emergency?"

"April's pissed off with me."

"That's it?" Heath scoffs and then starts laughing.

I frown at his reaction, wondering why it hurts so much, and don't bother saying anything. He's here now. That's enough. We don't need to talk. We can just be. I'm lucky to get this extra time with him this week. He dropped whatever he was doing to come and be with me. I'm grateful for that.

We pull into an empty parking lot next to a trail and he grabs my hand, leading me to a spot we've been to before. It's a little glade about five hundred meters off the main track. You kind of have to clamber through bush to get there, but then it pops up into this little patch of grass that's totally private.

Heath's moving kind of fast, his grip on my hand tight and urgent. I can't quite keep up with him and end up tripping over a tree root and whacking my knee.

"Ouch."

He hauls me back to my feet. "Come on, clumsy."

With a little laugh, he keeps tugging me along until we reach our haven.

As soon as he sits down, he yanks me onto his lap and starts kissing me. He sucks my neck and starts tugging at my sweater, unzipping it and releasing the top few buttons of my shirt so he can get easier access to my skin.

I let him, because I don't want to talk right now and this is what people in love do. They make love.

Heath told me that after our first time, which kind of took me by surprise, if I'm honest. We were just making out, and then all of a sudden his hands were everywhere and then he was on top of me and inside of me. It was like being on an express train, and I didn't have time to find the emergency brake.

It hurt and part of me didn't like it, but he kept whispering how great I felt and how much he loved me, so I kept my mouth shut. No guy has ever said those words to me before.

I mean, Dad would tell me that he loved me, but that's a completely different kind of love.

Afterward, Heath held me close like I was precious and told me that we'd just made love. Heath's my first boyfriend, and hopefully my last. That's what he tells me. We'll be together forever. It feels so good when he says stuff like that to me, so that's why I do the sex thing.

Even though it's illegal, which it won't be for long.

I'm still annoyed at Manu for bringing that to my attention.

Heath won't know about it either, and I'm not going to tell him.

As his fingers wiggle underneath my shirt and unclasp my bra, I remind myself that this is lovemaking. This is what you do when you care about someone, so I don't tell him that I'm not really in the mood. Once it's over, then we can talk.

He fondles me and I clench my teeth, April's words scouring my brain, images of Manu's concerned eyes flickering in the background.

"What's the matter?" Heath murmurs against my skin.

"Nothing," I mutter.

"Come on, get into it, then." He splays his hand across my back, pressing me against him. His hot mouth covers mine and I kiss him back, but I can't focus. And Heath can tell.

Leaning back with a huff, he scowls at me, his blue eyes looking dark and unfamiliar.

"I'm sorry." I cringe. "But I'm still feeling riled about this April thing." I'm not going to mention Manu. I don't want Heath getting annoyed that someone else knows about us. I've dealt with it, so he doesn't need to worry... or know.

My boyfriend tuts and rolls his eyes. "Just tell her you're sorry at school tomorrow. We need to keep her on our side or she could ruin this for us."

"I know."

"Why don't you invite her over or something? Or buy her a gift? Chocolates are always a good way to say sorry."

"Yeah, I guess." I tip my head and quietly murmur, "We're supposed to be going camping this weekend. I could ask her to come along to that."

His head jolts back, his eyes narrowing. "You're going away? This weekend? Where?"

"Some place Beck used to go as a kid. Dickey Flat, I think it's called. Just for two nights."

"Why didn't you tell me?"

I shrug. "I forgot."

"So I have to live without you for an entire weekend? I free up my time to be there for you for ballet, and you're only just telling me now that I don't need to?"

"I didn't think about it." I try for a smile. "When we're together, all I can really think about is you."

This barely appeases him. He lets out a harsh snicker. "And April, today, apparently."

I swallow.

He scoffs and shakes his head, pulling me in for a heated kiss. "Guess you better make it up to me, then."

Flipping me onto my back, he covers me. Dried leaves stick to my hair, and a twig is digging into my back as his weight pins me to the forest floor. He sucks my neck, lightly scraping my skin with his teeth when he nibbles my chin.

I jerk my head away without meaning to and he jolts back, another scowl on his face. "What is your problem today?"

I gaze at him, wondering why he's looking so different. There's a hard edge to him that I haven't seen before. Maybe I got a flash of it at the Four Square the other day, but he was just worried we might get caught.

What is he worried about now?

"You don't want this? You don't want me." He sits back, running his hand through his hair.

"Of course I do." I sit up, reaching for his face, but he bats my hand away. I curl it under my arm and fist my sweater. "Sorry. I'm just unsettled by this argument with April."

"Would you shut up about my stupid sister! I'm trying to make love to you here."

"I know. It's just, I... I texted you so I could talk about this."

"Since when do you ever want to talk?"

"I-I—"

"I can't believe you're making this all about you. Never mind me having to live without you for the weekend. What the hell am I supposed to do with my time?"

"Heath, I kind of have to go. It's expected—"

He snatches my arm, his fingers digging in as he gives it a hard yank.

"Ow," I whimper.

"Would you shut up about it? If you don't want to be with me, fine! Let's go." He stands up and storms off through the bush while I sit there reeling.

I don't know what just happened, but my fingers are trembling as I lightly brush a hand down my arm. I can still feel his fingers digging into my skin.

Why is he so mad at me?

I guess I should have told him about the camping trip. He's obviously hurt that I'm leaving him for the weekend. He needs to know that I don't want to, that I'd rather be with him.

Scrambling up, I chase after him, stumbling through the bush and running along the track.

"Heath!" I shout, panic taking me as I suddenly worry that he's left without me. I can't handle that. I need Heath. I can't go back to the way life was before. "Heath!" I practically scream, running off the track and finding him waiting by his car. He's lighting a cigarette. Sucking in some smoke, he leans against the car, looking slightly more relaxed.

Relief pounds through me, and I feel just a touch light-headed as I shuffle up to his car.

He flicks his gaze over me before taking another puff.

"I'm sorry I can't spend this weekend with you. I want to, but I have to go on this family thing. If I don't, they'll want to know why, and we're trying to keep us a secret."

Without a word, he leads me around to the passenger door and pops it open. "I guess this is the price I pay for dating a schoolgirl baby."

"I'm not a baby," I mutter.

He smirks. "You're my sexy little baby." He slaps my butt, hard. I gasp, but he just laughs and points at the seat. "Get in. I have to get going. I'll drop you home on my way."

I slip into the car, feeling like total shit. I hate the way Heath called me a baby. Why didn't I just keep my mouth shut and have sex with him? If we'd done that, he wouldn't be pissed, my arm wouldn't hurt, and my butt wouldn't be stinging. I could go away on this stupid camping trip this weekend knowing he'd be waiting for me on the other side of it.

Now I don't know what's going to happen.

Glancing sideways, I hunch farther down in my seat, staring out the window and trying to get my heart back to a normal rhythm that doesn't make me feel like throwing up.

17

STACEY

There's a chill vibe in the air as I stand at the sink, finishing off the dinner dishes. It's actually Tane's turn, but the guy has been inundated with homework lately, so I offered to take his chore tonight. I know, totally unlike me. I shocked the hell out of Harper when I offered, but I just need something to do with my hands, and I can't concentrate on school stuff anymore.

If you look into the living room, it's the perfect family snapshot. Beck's watching the news with Oscar and Rocket snuggled up beside him. Harper's reading a book while Cam and Bianca are playing a game of grab Scrabble. Bianca keeps giggling. It's a sweet sound, but it's grating on my nerves, because it makes me think of Hayden.

Why?

Because every freaking thing at the moment makes me think of Hayden.

Avoiding him at school is driving me crazy, but the idea of talking to him again is no better. It's like both of us don't want to have to deal with the nasty assumptions outside the gym or the fact that I accidentally checked out Mr. Hamilton when he walked past.

I close my eyes, my hands floating in the soapy water as I try to figure out what to do.

Grabbing the shepherd's pie dish, I use the scrubber to get the hard bits of cheese that stuck to the side during the grilling process. Man, it was good pie tonight. Harper is a seriously amazing cook. The smell of the delicious dish still lingers in the air as I frown, concentrating hard on the stubborn dirty spots.

After this, I need to head upstairs to proofread my assignment before submitting it. Then I'm going to sleep. If I can sleep. Everything's itchy and irritated—even my brain needs a good scratch—but I doubt it will alleviate the problem. In spite of the fact that I didn't actually see Hayden today, his face is crystal clear in my mind. I spent lunch with Luka and the girls playing netball again, trying to dodge thoughts of him. It was good to get some of my aggression out that way. It turned into a pretty fast-paced game, because some guys joined in and the girls were determined to win. It was actually really fun.

But it still didn't stop the Hayden bug. It crawled through my head for the entire day, and I'm not sure what—

The front door whips open, and I crane my body back to see what's going on. Willow storms in, slamming it shut behind her. Long straight hair flies off her shoulders as she practically runs for the stairs.

"Will?" Harper glances up from her book.

"I had a fight with April, and no, I don't want to talk about it!" She slams up the stairs and I step out of the kitchen, catching soapsuds off my hands as I look between everyone. We're all kind of wearing these similar perplexed expressions.

"Does one of us need to go and talk to her?" Beck murmurs.

Harper looks at the stairs, her face wrinkling with worry. "I don't know. Pushing her just makes her go silent. We probably need to let her process. She'll open up when she's ready. The counselor told me that she just needs patience and no pressure. If we push, she'll retreat. If we stand back with our arms open, then she'll be more likely to come forward and let us in."

I can tell by the expression on Harper's face that she really hates that.

"I get it," Cam murmurs from the table, tucking a lock

of hair behind his ear and sharing a meaningful smile with Bianca.

"Do you think she'll still want to come camping this weekend?" Oscar asks, looking kind of upset that the whole trip might be called off.

As much as I wish for that, I don't want to disappoint Ozzy or Beck, so I force a smile and quip, "She and April will probably be best friends again by the end of tomorrow."

Bianca giggles. "That's true. Camping's still on, Oz. Don't you worry."

Bianca winks at me like she's proud of me, and I head back into the kitchen to quickly finish up. I make sure the bench tops are clean and dry, the way Harper likes them—I refuse to be put through another *this is what I expect* lecture again. That girl is fussy when it comes to cleanliness.

"I'm just heading up to do some homework," I murmur to everyone before disappearing up the stairs. Pausing at the top, I can hear Willow sniffling and seriously have to resist the urge to go check on her, but I don't want to do that pushing pressure thing and make her curl into a little porcupine ball. Hopefully she'll feel better in the morning.

Hopefully I will too.

18

WILLOW

I've had a super shitty day. After basically no sleep, I woke up feeling like death. The only small relief was the fact that Harper didn't try to solve any of my problems.

"I'm here for you if you need me, sis. Always. If you want to talk through your argument with April, I'm here for you."

I appreciate that, like a lot. Because the truth is, I'll never be able to tell her why I was really crying last night. She'll never understand about Heath.

Just like April doesn't seem to either.

She ignored me all day today, and I didn't exactly put in much effort, either. I don't want it to slip that Heath is super pissed I have to go away this weekend. I don't want to tell her that he slapped me really hard on the butt. That's private, and I'm not exactly sure what to do about it. I love Heath so much. I'd be totally lost without him. I guess in relationships, you just have to put up with a few things you don't like.

The sex is getting easier. It doesn't hurt anymore, and it always puts Heath in a great mood, so it's worth it. As for the bum-smacking thing, well, maybe if he ever does it again, I'll just need to really nicely say that I don't like it.

I swallow, feeling kind of sick.

"Enjoy ballet." Tane gives me a tired smile.

He is so ready for the end of term. The guy's been pulling a couple of late nights to get assignments done. Harper's been helping him a little, but it's still *his* work that he needs to turn in.

"Thanks for the ride." I pop the door open.

"Harper will pick you up at five thirty."

"Okay." I slip out of the car. Forcing a smile is really hard work, but thankfully Tane drives away quickly. He's on milking with Beck and Linc tonight, and he can't afford to be too late. He's doing Harper a favor by dropping me at ballet.

Pivoting on my foot, I head toward the old church, wondering what to do with myself. I doubt Heath will show up to hang with me. He gave me no indication when he dropped me home yesterday that he'd be here.

I gnaw on the inside of my cheek, wishing this sick feeling in my stomach would go away. I guess I'll just have to loiter around behind the fence, playing some lame game on my phone.

It's not my official lesson today, not that I'd dance if it was.

I mean, I guess I kind of miss moving my body sometimes, feeling that music flow through me, but ballet was always so restrictive. Everything had to be perfect, and it drove me nuts.

Memories of Dad suddenly flood me, his proud smile as he waited for me outside of class four times a week. He'd pick me up on his way home from work, and as soon as I saw him, I'd skip out of the dance studio.

"Hey, fairy princess." He'd gather me in his arms and swing me around. It didn't matter how big I got or how much older I was, he'd still do it and I always loved it.

As soon as we were settled into his car and our seat belts were buckled, he'd put on Tchaikovsky or Mozart and say the same thing every time.

"Okay. Talk ballet to me, princess. Confuse and inspire me with your French."

I'd giggle and go into detail explaining each move from the class, feeding off his pride and enthusiasm. He'd let me complain if I needed to or be a little smug if I'd nailed something I'd been working on.

"Ah, *ma belle fille*." His finger would pop into the air with triumph. "I'm so proud of you for owning that *fouette*."

I'd giggle. "I don't own it, Dad. I just managed to do *one* decent one today. I'll keep working on it, though. That move is mine, and I'm going to master it by the end of the year."

"Of that, I am sure."

He loved my determination and had no idea it was all for him. He always believed in me, so that's why I danced. I had this plan to do one more year of intense ballet, then tell my parents I needed to pull back so I could focus on my studies. Education was important to them, so even though they probably would have been disappointed, I knew they'd understand.

But I never got the chance to do that. In some ways, it's a blessing I could avoid that awkward conversation.

A blessing?

Am I insane? Am I somehow implying that their deaths are a blessing?

I suddenly hate myself with a white-hot rage that makes me shudder.

Struggling to walk past the brick building, I try to fight off that empty pain in my chest. It hurts to breathe, to swallow. To exist.

I miss you! I miss you so much!

I brush a hand down my face, trying to figure out what I'll do for the next ninety minutes. I'll go insane if I can't get images of Dad out of my head. It's like this sweet torture. I simultaneously love and hate the memories.

Is it too much to hope that Heath will be here to make it all better?

I round the corner, my breath on hold until I spot him leaning against the fence. His tie is flapping just a little in the wind, and he smooths it down, smiling when he notices me.

Relief gushes through me, the very sight of Heath obliterating the painful memories and filling me with… something. I don't even know what it is, but the empty feeling eases every time I'm around him.

Rushing forward with a smile, I stop by the fence and check out the box of chocolates he's holding.

He hands them to me with a sheepish smile. "I'm sorry we fought yesterday. I didn't mean to snap at you. I was just disappointed that I wasn't going to get to see you."

I brush my hand over the shiny packet, struggling to speak.

"You have no idea how much I think about you. All the time. I just want to be with you, touch you, hold you… all the time." His husky whisper sends a thrill from my neck to my knees.

My heart feels warm, that empty feeling evaporating completely. Slipping my hand into his, I check that no one's watching as he leads me around the corner to the secluded parking spot he always chooses. He looks around as well, and once we're sure we're alone, we lean together for a gentle kiss. It's delicate and sweet and restores all my faith in him.

"I love you, Willow."

His expression is so sweet, and my lips wobble into a smile. "I love you too."

Pulling me into a hug, he glues our bodies together, and for a moment, I revel in the secure sensation. But then he pulls away and tugs me to his car.

I don't know what he has planned for us, but I just have to go with it. We're making up. We're putting yesterday behind us. Heath is sweet and gentle. I love him.

And I'm super surprised when he ends up pulling into his own driveway.

Maybe April's not home this afternoon. That's weird. She usually is. Unlike her parents. They're never around. Their dad's a pilot, and he's constantly overseas or sleeping. Their mum is... well, I don't know what she does. I saw her once when I was walking through the house, but April didn't bother introducing me to her.

"What are we doing here?" I unbuckle my seat belt.

Heath sighs and pats my leg. "You should talk to April. Tell her how grateful you are for her help. Invite her camping. That'll make her feel better."

"Are you sure?" I can't help my surprise. I was seriously going to avoid all mention of camping because I didn't want to aggravate him, and now he's the one bringing it up.

"Yeah. I was thinking about it last night. You have to go, right? So you may as well have a friend there with you. Someone to watch over you. I wish it could be me."

"Me too." I lay my hand over his.

He squeezes my knee. "In a couple of years, the gap won't seem so big. People will understand." He gently kisses me, then spins to open his door. "Come on. It'll be okay."

I ease into the house, Heath pushing my back and taking me up the stairs. I kind of need him to, because my legs have turned to silly string. What am I supposed to say?

What—

"Go on." Heath knocks on April's door and darts away, leaving me standing there to face her on my own.

It's probably the right thing to do.

April and her brother aren't exactly mates. Just the sight of him seems to aggravate her. It's actually totally surprising that Heath wants me to take her along, but he obviously likes the idea of someone watching out for me. How sweet is that?

The door eases open, and April's lips part with surprise. "What are you doing here?"

"Um…" I lick my lips. "Well, I wanted to… I'm sorry, okay? I hate things being off between us. I don't like it when you're angry with me."

April doesn't move for a moment, and I'm wondering if she's about to slam the door in my face, but then she sighs and pulls it open so I can step into her orderly bedroom.

It's all pastel colors and soft, neat lines. Even her pinboard has an ordered quality about it—each note and photograph at perfect right angles to the next. I love that.

Taking a seat on the end of her bed, I cross my ankles and fidget with my bag strap.

"I know you don't like me and Heath together, and I'm sorry that I'm not willing to break up with him. I love him."

"I know." April huffs.

"And he loves me."

"Yep." April nods and won't look at me.

"I've missed you at school. I hate not hanging out together."

Closing her eyes, April sniffs and crosses her arms. "I hate it too. I guess I've just been really annoyed that all you ever want to do is be with Heath or talk about him. It's like you're obsessed, and I… I want my friend back. I want to hang out with you too. Not always just at school."

My lips curl into a grin. "How about this weekend?"

"Oh, yeah?" She seems a little skeptical, and I can't wait to wipe that look off her face.

With an excited grin, I grab her hand and tell her. "Yes. I'm going on a family camping trip, and I'm allowed to invite a friend."

"That's right. I remember you telling me that. I thought you didn't want to go."

"Well, I kinda don't, but if you come with me, then I think I'll have a good time."

"You sure?" April's expression still hasn't lost that skepticism. "You honestly want me to come?"

"Yes! Of course I do."

"You wouldn't rather have Heath?"

I let out a breathy laugh, nearly joking that he's not

even an option anyway, but I swallow back the words before they tumble out. I don't want to offend her.

Instead I reach for her hand and pull her down to sit next to me. "I really want to go with *you*. I know my family will be there, but it'll be like a whole weekend just the two of us. Girl time. Everyone wants to meet you, so it's perfect."

"They want to meet me?"

"Yeah! Of course they do! They want to know who this April girl is that I talk about all the time."

"You talk about me?"

"Well, duh. You're my best friend." I laugh and pull her into a hug. "I really want you there."

"Okay." I hear the smile in her voice as she grips me back.

"Thank you for being such a good friend," I whisper, meaning it one hundred percent.

She obviously appreciates the comment, because when she leans back, her eyes are glistening a little.

A soft knock on the door makes her flinch, and she glances up. Heath's leaning against the frame, smiling at us. "I need to get you back. It's only a short class today."

"Yeah." I stand, smoothing a hand over my hair and

glancing down at April. "Have fun packing. We can pick you up on Saturday morning."

"I'll drop her off," Heath offers, his smile still in place.

April's eyes narrow slightly, but she doesn't say anything, and I head for the door and a quick exit. The vibe is good. We need to keep it that way.

Bouncing down the steps, I slip into the car and smile at Heath as he reverses back out onto the road.

"So, she said yes?"

"Yep." I grin. "Thanks so much for making me ask her. I so needed to."

"I just figured since I can't be there, at least someone I know will be there with you."

"Yeah." I nod, not sure why that statement doesn't sit as good as it did before.

When we reach his secret parking spot, he cuts the engine and runs around to my door so he can capture me against him as soon as I step out of it.

My giggle is swallowed by his mouth as he dives toward me, heating my bones with a passionate kiss. His arms wrap around me like he never wants to let me go.

Running my hand over the fuzz on his head, I pull back for a breather, laughing when he dives straight in for another kiss.

"How am I going to live without you?" he murmurs against my cheek.

I lean into the hug, resting my chin on his shoulder. "I'll be back on Monday, so I can see you again on Tuesday. Ballet continues through the holidays."

He trails kisses up to my ear and then down my neck. "You need to find lots of excuses to see April. Maybe arrange a sleepover or something." He sucks my neck and pulls the neck of my leotard so he can access a little more skin. "I'll need you when you get back."

I smile, loving the idea of being needed.

His hands continue to run over me, and when he pushes me flat against his car, I can feel his excitement. Thankfully we don't have time for that right now.

But he's going to want me to make time as soon as I get back.

I can see it in his eyes when he leans away to look at me. I give him a tentative smile.

His eyes are so hungry, his hands so strong. It scares me a little, but mostly thrills me. I'm wanted. I'm needed.

That's a good thing.

My watch alarm starts beeping, and Heath growls in his throat before laying one more rough and heady kiss against my mouth. He pulls away just as fast, jumping in his car and speeding down the road.

I wipe my lips, hoping they aren't too swollen. Harper will be here any moment.

Running to the usual meeting point, I hitch the bag on my shoulder and wait for my sister, wondering why that sick feeling is back in my stomach again.

19

HAYDEN

In spite of the fact that it's Friday, I slump out of school, my feet scuffing the ground as I turn right to make my way home. I should be elated like most of the student body. Two weeks of freedom!

But I'm a dead weight, heavy limbs carting me along the footpath.

A noise behind me catches my attention, and I spin around to see Cam, Manu and Tane joshing around. Cam's got Manu in a friendly headlock. Manu's giggling his high-pitched laugh while Tane musses up his reckless curls. Wriggling free, Manu and Cam have a friendly scrap, their shirts coming free as they tussle and laugh. Schoolbags gets dumped on the ground, and people coming out of the building snicker at the show.

I watch them horsing over to Tane's car so they can no doubt wait for the girls.

It's hard not to sink even lower as I watch these manly guys attracting all this attention. Good attention. Not the kind of attention I gain when I sing in the hallways or get excited and my voice goes high.

No one laughs and smiles at me the way they're laughing and smiling at the rugby boys. No wonder Stacey wants to keep us a secret.

"Us," I scoff, shaking my head.

What us?

I tut, misery clinging to me like ivy. Camping's going to suck. Maybe I should just bail.

But Bianca was so excited when I saw her at lunchtime. She's convinced this trip will be the resolution Stacey and I need. We've basically avoided each other all week. There's been so many times I've wanted to walk up and apologize, but something stops me every time. Maybe I'm subconsciously waiting for this weekend, like it will somehow be my magical moment to make things right between us.

I hope it works.

I miss her.

Which means I really do have to go camping.

Besides, what else am I going to do? Hole up in my room watching romantic movies? I know that's what I'll end up doing. What is it about wanting to salt wounds with romantic songs and movies? It's like a bizarre kind of torture I can't resist.

"Have a great break!" The student PE teacher waves to a bunch of students as he pulls out of the parking lot. They wave back like he's a celebrity, and it only makes me feel worse. He is pretty dreamy. And I'm pretty not.

Picking up my pace, I end up breaking into a run and arrive home sweaty and flustered. I hope I have the house to myself. I want a long shower and maybe a cup of coffee before I can contemplate packing.

But no such luck.

As I turn into my driveway, I spot Dad's feet on the garage ladder, the top half of his body up in the roof space.

Wandering over to him, I look up and mumble, "Hey, Dad. What are you doing?"

"Aw, hey, mate. Take this, will ya?" He hands down a blue bedroll, and I drop it on the floor by my feet before reaching back to grab the tent. We do this for the next few minutes as he passes down all of our camping boxes.

Finally he climbs down to join me and surveys the gear with a happy grin. "We haven't used this stuff in ages. I wanted to check it was still in good nick for you."

I lightly kick the tent and nod.

"You remember everything I taught you boys about good camping, right?"

"Yeah." Crouching down, I pop open the box with the orange lid and finger the survival kit Dad put together for Christmas one year. Pulling out the pocketknife, I flick it open, checking the blade is clean before picking up the compass and then the flint. "Will I really need this stuff? It's not like we're going bush. It's a big group of us, at a campsite."

"Well, maybe not, but where's the fun if you don't take a bit of this stuff with you? You could always go off trail for a little adventure." His eyes twinkle with excitement, and I start to wonder if I should tell him to go instead of me.

"I spoke to Beck yesterday."

I jerk to my feet. "You did?"

"Yeah. Happened to bump into him at Mitre 10. He was in the line behind me when I was giving my account details, and he heard my last name. As I was walking away, he asked me if I knew a Hayden Thorp. It was great to meet the guy. Feel like you'll be in good hands, but want you to be prepared for yourself as well."

I sigh and bob my head as Dad goes through everything with me.

He seems really happy that I'm off to do something

rugged and manly. And here was me thinking I was just going to try and repair my relationship with Stacey.

"I told Beck you've got plenty of experience and he doesn't need to worry about you. That seemed to perk him up a bit. He's taking a fair few of you. It's a big responsibility."

"We'll be okay."

"Oh, I know you will. You're a Thorp." He smacks me on the arm, always harder than he means to, and I can't help a small wince.

Dad's expression falters and he gives the spot a rub, silently apologizing.

The doubt on his face right now hurts worse than my arm.

"You'll, uh, you'll make us proud, right, mate? Show the others what you're capable of?"

I swallow and Dad runs a hand over his bald head, obviously finding this conversation way awkward. Well, maybe he should just stop talking, then!

"Beck mentioned that the twin girls have never been bush camping before. They're not used to roughing it. This is a great opportunity for you to really step up and, you know, show them how awesome you are."

I bob my head, because I don't know what to say.

Is Dad implying that I'm only awesome when I'm building a fire or pitching a tent?

He wraps his arm around my shoulders and gives me a squeeze. "I'm, uh… well, yeah."

And with that, he pats me on the back, and what he probably considers a really great heart-to-heart is over.

I watch him stride out of the garage, calling over his shoulder, "Let me unearth the pack from under my bed. We'll cram as much stuff as we can into that thing."

Gazing down at the plethora of camping gear, I lightly kick the tent again. Dad's chat felt like drinking a glass full of stones. They're now lodged in my digestive tract, painful and weighing a freaking tonne.

Let's hope I can prove my worth this weekend.

With an irritated tut, I shake my head and start to dread tomorrow even more than I did before.

20

STACEY

T he sky is a dull gray today. It's like it's warning us not to go. I shiver and rub my jacket sleeves, hovering on the porch while Cam, Tane and Manu load up the cars with all our gear.

Hayden and Bianca are kind of helping, but they keep stopping to lean their heads together and whisper things. Things about me, no doubt.

Grrrr.

Why did she invite him?

He glances over at me, and we lock eyes for the briefest moment. His lips rise with just the hint of a sad smile before he turns back to lift a bag and pass it to Cam.

I walk back into the house to fill my takeaway cup with more coffee. I'm going to *need* it to get through today. Beck's voice filters through the kitchen window.

"If there's any problems, check in with the neighbors. There's no phone reception where we're going, but I've told Bob to be available if you need him. And thanks for looking after Rocket. I could take him, but it's just another thing to keep an eye on."

"No worries, mate. I've got this covered. You just go away and relax."

Beck kind of scoffs. "You've seen how many kids I'm taking, right?"

Linc laughs and I scowl, a little insulted by how adults always think of us "kids" as such a pain in the ass. I wait for the machine to finish with my coffee, tapping my fingers on the hard countertop. Come on!

I can't shake the grumpy vibes as I secure the lid and walk back outside. Willow and her friend April are on the porch when I step out the door. Their heads are ducked together too, and I want to snap at them that it's rude to whisper in front of people.

But I press my lips together, trying to hold it all in.

I don't want to go on this stupid trip.

Camping is so not my thing, not to mention the fact that at some point, I'll no doubt have to have a proper conversation with Hayden.

But what do I say to him?

My heart hurts.

I'm tired.

I don't want to do this.

"All right." Beck walks out of the house, clapping his hands and looking pretty pumped.

Ugh.

I turn away from him as he walks past me and thrusts his hand in April's direction.

"Beckett Connell, and you must be April?"

"Yes." She stands up with a nervous grin, wiping her hands on the side of her jeans.

"Nice to meet you." He smiles while they shake hands. "I was hoping to say hi to your mum or dad, but they just dropped and ran, did they?"

April darts her eyes to Willow before answering. "Dad's flying to Dubai and then on to London. He was in a hurry to get to the airport."

"Oh really? Why's he flying all the way over there?"

"He's a pilot."

"Very nice."

"And Mum's busy today. Hair appointment and shopping and stuff, so she couldn't drop me."

"Do you have any other family?"

April looks to the side again while Willow crosses her arms and is so obviously trying to be casual.

I frown as I study them. My lie detector is buzzing.

April shakes her head and swallows. "No. Just me."

"Well, I'm glad you can come with us. Keep you entertained while your parents are so busy."

A smile pulls her lips wide, and she glances up at Beck, this fleeting look crossing her face.

Is it longing? Admiration?

Like maybe she wishes she had a dad just like Beck?

"Hopefully I can catch your mum when I drop you home." He winks and April swallows, sharing a nervous glance with Willow, who gives her a tight smile. Beck doesn't seem to notice because he's distracted by Manu trying to juggle plastic cups and dropping them in the dirt. "Oi! We have to drink out of those, mate!"

Manu scrambles to pick them up as Beck marches over to him, but I keep staring at the girls. Willow's eyeing Manu with a scowl while April plays with the end of her very stubby ponytail. Half of it's falling out because it's not really long enough to tie back yet. She must be growing it out, like me.

Talk about awkward.

If there was some formula, I'd take it.

My hair looks heinous at the moment, and I haven't had Hayden around to help me with it either.

This sucks!

I miss him.

Blinking, I glance at my best friend and almost wish he'd look my way so I could smile at him. Something.

I can't go into this trip acting like a grumpy cow. I need to make this right with Hayden. But how?

"Hey, Will, have you remembered to call ballet and let them know you can't make the classes this weekend?" Harper glances up from her phone, like she's checking off some "to do" list before we can leave.

"Yep." Willow grabs April's hand and skips over to the white wagon, slipping into the back seat and shutting the door.

I stand there uselessly, trying to figure out which car I'll be traveling in. Bianca slips into Cam's ute with Hayden and Manu in the back.

"You coming, Stace?" Cam waves me over.

My stomach clenches, but it's not like I can make a scene in front of everyone. Looks like I'll be traveling in the back with the boys. Tane's already started up the white wagon with Harper in the passenger seat, and Beck's got Oscar and his friend, Mike, in his ute.

Holding my breath, I slip into the window seat. Poor

Hayden's squished in the middle. He gives me a closed-mouth smile when I glance at him, then sniffs and pulls something out of his bag.

It's my favorite snack—two white-chocolate raspberry muffins.

"Shelley was baking yesterday."

I gaze down at the precious token, my lips rising into a smile. "Thank you."

"I would have brought one for everyone, but I was only allowed to steal two."

"Do you want one?" I hold them up.

"Nah." Hayden shakes his head. "I got them for you."

"I'll have one." Manu sticks out his hand.

"Forget it." I frown at him.

He gives me a sad face while Hayden can't fight his grin. I nudge him with my elbow.

"Thanks." We share our first smile in what feels like forever as Cam reverses and takes off after Tane. Beck brings up the rear of the convoy. I glance out the back window and watch his ute bump down the uneven driveway.

"I'm sorry about this week," Hayden softly murmurs. "I'm sorry if you don't want me here, but I've really missed you. Maybe we can figure out what… what we're doing… over the weekend?"

I gaze into his beautiful gray eyes, my insides vibrating like an earthquake is running through me. "Yeah, okay."

This seems to satisfy him, and he leans back, gazing out the front as Bianca pumps up the music and starts singing. Cam tries to join in, which sounds freaking awful and gives Manu and Bianca the giggles. This just makes him sing louder, and soon I'm struggling not to crack up as well.

Hayden is cringing like he's listening to metal scraping against metal, and eventually starts singing as well, just to counter it. Manu joins in too, sounding… well, not too bad, actually. Who knew? The guy's definitely got rhythm. He's tapping out a beat on his knee while he tries to counter Cam's awful singing.

I guess I may as well join in too.

I'm not the world's best singer, but I've got to be better than Cam, surely!

Punching out the lyrics, I glance at Hayden, who gives me one of those awkward, cringy smiles. I wrinkle my nose at him and start singing that much louder. And soon the car is filled with this weird disjointed sound as three nightingales compete with two squawking seagulls.

HAYDEN

I t took just over an hour to get to Dickey Flat, which sped by super fast thanks to Cam's singing, Manu's tapping, and the delightful sound of Bianca and Stacey's laughter. It felt like old times again, and when we pulled in and parked next to the white family wagon, we were all in high spirits.

The sun had come out to play, taking the chill out of the air and making me feel like summer was thinking about returning over the next few months.

Fine by me.

I love the heat.

And so does Stace.

I watch her chatting with Bianca as we wait for Beck to pull in with the ute.

There's hardly anyone around. I scan the other cars—a blue Ford, a dirt-covered van and a red-hot Honda civic.

"Looks like we'll have the pick of the lot." Beck grins as he walks over to us. Rubbing his hands together, he takes a deep breath, obviously feeling pretty happy. I haven't seen his smile quite so big before. "Let's go for a wander and pick a spot. Then we can come back and get the gear."

We trail after the big guy and wander past the two boulders that signify the entrance to the camping area. This place is really beautiful. There's an idyllic river meandering by on the left and every shade of green you can imagine. Tall trees border the camping area, some of them green, some starting to blossom, and a few still naked from the winter season. We walk the narrow, undulating dirt path, surveying patches of flat grass to our left and right.

Beck eventually decides that the huge flat area on the right will be perfect. I could tell he kind of wanted the one on the left, closer to the river, but a group of tents is already there.

"Let's pitch in a circle formation, all pointing in toward each other, and not too close to the path."

"Where's the bathroom?" Stacey wiggles her legs, and Beck points to a hill behind us.

"Up there. Long drops."

Stacey's expression flatlines. "Excuse me?"

"Long drop toilets."

"Ah, gross."

"Ah, camping." Beck winks at her and strides past. "Meet us at the cars once you're done. Let's get our site set up."

Stacey makes a gagging face and I snicker, shooting her a sympathetic smile. She swallows convulsively and heads up the hill, with Bianca in tow, while we troop back to the cars.

Beck has us line up, and we unload one vehicle at a time. It's a hell of a lot of stuff considering we're only here for two nights, but I guess that's camping. I carry the weighty pack, wondering what the heck Stacey put in here. She obviously doesn't know the meaning of "pack light." Dropping the bag at my feet, I run back to help Manu with the chilly bin. We bought two of them. With this many people, you need a lot of food. And these chillies are like industrial. We've got one at home. They keep the food cold for way longer than the standard one you might take to a barbecue.

With a grunt, we place it down in the middle of the camping area.

"Yeah, good. Thanks, boys." Beck unzips the first tent

bag. "Right, I'll be in this one with Oscar and Mike. Oi! You two! Come over here and help." He calls the younger boys back before they can sneak off to throw a rugby ball around.

They groan and jog back as Beck starts pointing out where he wants everyone and who's sleeping where.

"It's boys on this side, girls in that half of the circle. I don't want to find anyone in the wrong tent, if you catch my drift." He eyeballs Cam, who raises his hands, blinking innocently while Bianca goes so beet red her freckles disappear.

Crouching down, I start unzipping my small tent. It says two-person on the side, but it's so much better with only one. I don't know how two people would fit comfortably in this thing. Dad bought it for me a few Christmases ago. We've done the camping thing every year since before I can remember. Admittedly, it's usually in the summer, but I'm game to try an early spring experience.

I manage to pitch my tent quickly and am the first one done. Rolling up the bag and spare pegs, I then wander over to Stacey, who is obviously struggling. Cam's come over to assist the twins, who have no idea what they're doing.

"Yep, make sure it's tight first. Okay, now put the pegs in."

I run up to help them peg in the base while Cam grabs out the poles and starts clipping them together.

"You guys never camped before?" I ask Stacey.

She shakes her head. "We've always been a resort holiday kind of family."

"Nice." I wiggle my eyebrows at her. "My parents have been dragging me out every year since before I can remember."

"I'm guessing they were wise enough to do it in the summer." Stacey shoots a dark look over her shoulder at Beck.

I follow her line of sight in time to see Beck throw back his head with a loud laugh. I don't know what Tane just said, but it's obviously tickled Beck's fancy.

"Look at his face, Stace," I murmur.

She does, and her expression softens. "He's been working so hard. It's nice to see him more relaxed, I guess. I just don't know why I have to be here for it."

"I'm glad you are." I wink at her and she smiles, then starts blinking and looks to the ground.

I turn my focus back to Cam and continue helping him put up the tent for the girls.

Bianca follows his instructions, obviously eager to learn while a not-so-keen Stacey loiters on the sidelines, stepping in occasionally to hold something. The dome tent is soon up and stable.

Bianca's stoked, her smile like a child's on Christmas morning. "This is so cool." She climbs into the tent, laughing. "Stace, get in here!"

Her twin sister pulls a face before ducking inside to look around. Their sneakers stick out the entrance while Cam and I share a grin.

How cute are they?

"Did they bring bedrolls to sleep on?" Cam asks Beck when he wanders over to check on us.

"Uh, I'll put them on a double airbed. It's around here somewhere."

"There." I spot it and head over, grabbing the hand pump at the same time.

Cam and I take turns pumping up the girls' air mattress. It's not too much of a mission when you're working with Mr. Muscle. I'm kind of glad it's not summer so I don't have to check out his guns—more like cannons—every time he pumps air into the mattress.

My twigs would look so tiny and small beside him. Thank God for cooler weather and jackets.

Manu's pitchy giggle catches my ear, and I glance over

as he and Tane finish up the bigger tent for the boys. It's nice they invited him to join. He doesn't have any other family that I know of. Just his mum, who must have had him pretty young. Stacey reckons she got pregnant in high school. I haven't seen the woman, but I've heard she's a tough nugget.

I can't help smiling as I watch Manu dancing around like a monkey. I don't know what brought it on, but Harper and Tane are cracking up. Manu is good for a laugh. He gets in trouble a bit at school and he's kind of reckless, but he's a good guy. He may be considered a bad boy, but he's not a bully.

"Here you go, ladies." Cam finishes tightening the stopper and starts feeding a nice, firm airbed into the tent.

"Thanks, babe. This is so cool."

Cam grins at Bianca's enthusiasm. Her smile is so bright and beautiful when she steps out of the tent. Cam drapes his arm over her shoulders and kisses the top of her head.

Meanwhile, Stacey stands next to me, glancing my way for a microsecond before angling her body away from me.

I wonder if she'll ever let me drape my arm over her shoulders and give her a kiss.

It's obviously not in the cards this weekend.

I swallow, trying to come to terms with my disappointment. Maybe I shouldn't have come on this trip. But the car ride was fun. She's smiled at me a couple of times.

That's hopeful, right?

Too bad the feeling is so fleeting.

"Race ya!" Oscar starts running, a rugby ball tucked against his side.

Mike laughs and bounds after him. "Kick it! Kick it!" He gets his hands ready as Oscar boots the ball into the air.

"Oi! You two. You're not done!" Beck shouts from the entrance of their tent, but they ignore him, laughing wildly as Mike does a high kick that arches to the right. The ball lands like a grenade in the middle of the other campers' circle.

"Boys!" Beck storms over as someone emerges from the biggest tent to see what's going on. It's a tall, good-looking guy, and I recognize him immediately.

My heart sinks so fast I'm pretty sure it's nestled into my heels.

"Oh, hey, it's Mr. Hamilton." Cam grins and waves at him.

I glance sideways to look at Stacey, and sure enough,

she's starting to blush. She smiles and waves as well when he picks up the rugby ball and wanders over.

Oh great, he's coming to say hello.

Locking my jaw, I head back to my tent, determined not to be a part of the friendly howdy-doody. Crouching down by my bag, I get busy unrolling my little sleeping mat and setting out my sleeping bag and pillow.

"What are you guys doing here?" Mr. Hamilton laughs.

"Beck wanted to come camping, so we came camping," Stacey answers.

"Who's Beck?"

"That's me." He steps up, and there's probably a hand-shake of some kind going on. I refuse to look. "I'm guardian to this lot, and this is our first official camping trip."

"In the winter," Stacey snips. "Camping in the winter."

"According to the calendar, spring has officially start-ed," Bianca says.

"Whatever. It's freezing."

"Aw, come on. There's nothing like camping in the crisp, fresh air like this. Spring's the best time to come out here." Mr. Hamilton chuckles.

"I agree." Beck sounds pretty happy that he's got the backup of the student teacher.

The friendly chatter continues on behind me, the geniality of it all making my skin crawl.

Bloody Mr. Hamilton.

Why did he have to be here? Of all the freaking places in New Zealand he could camp, it had to be Dickey Flat.

It just had to be!

22

WILLOW

I stay near the tent I'll be sharing with April and Harper, watching Mr. Hamilton's friendly smile as he shakes hands with Beck and says hi to everyone.

"Here you go." April hands me another peg, and I walk around to the back corner of the tent to secure the last guy rope.

We've done a pretty good job pitching the tent. Harper and I have been camping every summer since Oscar was about three. I used to love it, which is why I'm so surprised by how painful pitching this tent has been today. I mean, it was easy to do, but it hurt the entire time. The deep black hole inside of me writhed and ached every step of the way. Because Dad's not here directing us. It used to annoy the heck out of Harper, the way he'd hover around, checking each step as we went.

"That's it, girls. Just a little tighter in that corner."

"Dad!" Harper would complain. "We've done this a hundred times."

"A poorly pitched tent will bite you in the butt later, Caramel. I just want you to have a good experience."

She'd roll her eyes while Dad and I shared a grin.

Caramel. That was his nickname for Harper.

She'll never get called that again.

And I'll never be anyone's fairy princess again. Never ever.

My eyes burn, the pain in my chest so immense. I stand up, pushing the heel of my hand into my sternum. I need Heath. I need him distracting me, feeding me liquor and cigarettes, helping me to relax. I wish I wasn't here. Why did I have to come? Why didn't I make more of an effort to get out of it?

Heath wants me with him.

He needs me!

And I'm stuck here, my chest hurting as I pitch a stupid tent that I don't even want to sleep in!

"Just call me Justin." Mr. Hamilton's voice distracts me. I glance up to see his broad smile. "We're not in school right now, you guys. It's the holidays." He winks, and I'm pretty sure Stacey is blushing right now. "I don't know everyone's names." He points around the circle, each person taking a turn to introduce themselves.

Hayden emerges from his little pup tent, and Mr. Hamilton points at him. "Do you go to North Ridge too?"

Hayden works his jaw to the side and nods. "Yeah."

"And how are you related to this mob?" Mr. Hamilton asks with a friendly smile.

Stacey jumps in before Hayden can even open his mouth. "He's our friend. Bianca and me. We're friends. We hang out at lunch sometimes."

Stacey glances over her shoulder and smiles at Hayden. His lips rise, barely, and when she spins back, his face completely morphs with this gutted kind of frown.

Bianca's gazing at him, looking sad, as well. What's going on there?

You know what, I actually don't care.

I rub my shoulder and force my mind back to Heath, walking around to the back of the tent to find his sister. At least she's here. It eases the pain a little.

April's pulling out a sleeping mat, and I crouch down to find mine as well.

"Do you think Mr. Hamilton's cute? All the other girls seem to. Did you see Stacey with her goo-goo eyes?"

I glance at April and shrug. "He's pretty good-looking, I guess. I can see why the girls like him."

April wrinkles her nose as she stands, peering around our tent for another glimpse of him. "He's not my type. Out of all the guys here this weekend, I think Manu's the hottest."

"Manu?" I step up behind her to check him out. I was so annoyed when I found out he was coming. It was only yesterday that Tane mentioned it, and it took everything in me to hold my composure and not freak out. Manu—the biggest threat to my relationship with Heath—was coming camping. I barely slept a wink last night, but decided that as long as I stay as far away from him as possible this weekend, then hopefully we'll have no chance to talk and nothing will get said that might be overheard. I'm not getting busted by that idiot.

I study his long body. He's taller than Tane, which surprises me, I've always thought of him as the shorter, kid brother type of friend, but there you go. He's in between Tane and Cam in height. He's skinnier though, and his hair is such a mess. Always a mess. It's like it's never been introduced to a brush, like ever. His reckless black curls are all over the place, although some of them have got bleach on the tips, like he wanted to try an experiment and it backfired. It looks weird and doesn't suit his face, if you ask me. You can tell he has Maori blood running through his veins. His dark skin and the shape of his face—I can picture him in traditional Maori dress, brandishing a taiaha or a patu, doing one of those war dances or a haka. He'd be fierce in battle, I can tell.

"I think he's super hot," April murmurs. "And I'd take him over Mr. HellaYum any day."

I glance at April's face, an idea forming so quickly it's impossible to hide my smile. Maybe it's providence that she and Manu both came along this weekend. Quiet, shy, sweet April. What better way to make her weekend awesome than to set her up with a guy she thinks is super hot?

And imagine if it totally worked out?

It'd be the best distraction for her, and I could hang out with Heath guilt free, because April would be so busy being in love with Manu that she wouldn't need me to spend weekends with her anymore. I wouldn't feel like I was ditching her or trying to divide my time to keep them both happy.

I bite the inside of my cheek, excitement trilling through me. I love this.

Walking out from around the tent, I pull April along behind me, approaching the circle, just as Mr. Hamilton says, "A couple of my mates were thinking of going for a hike across the bridges and through that tunnel. There's a great spot, really beautiful, just beyond the tunnel. Did you guys bring torches? You're welcome to join them." He points over his shoulder and then waves a couple of his mates over. "This is Deek and Terry."

They wander over and say hi, raising their hands to wave and smile at everyone.

"I'd be keen." Cam grins.

Bianca bobs on her toes. "Me too."

"All right." Mr. Hamilton smiles. "You guys want to grab your stuff and we'll get organized. I thought I'd stick around here for a game of touch if you want to join." He directs the question at Mike and Oscar, who share an excited grin, obviously enamored by the dynamic student teacher.

They gaze, starry-eyed, as he and his mates jog back to their tents while Beck rounds us up before we take off.

"So, anyone else going with Cam and Bianca?"

Manu raises his hand, so I shoot mine into the air too. April double glances at me, then tentatively raises hers.

"Five of you then. Okay, right." Beck claps his hands together. "Here's how this weekend is going to work. If you want to go do something—fine, but you have to check in with me first. Once you're finished with that activity, you then return to camp to check in with me, or someone else if I'm not here, before going off to do anything else. There's no cell phone reception, so we have to do it old school, communicating face-to-face with our mouths and stuff. I know that's scary, but—"

"Ha-ha." Stacey rolls her eyes while Bianca and Cam laugh.

Beck grins. "Just remember to look after each other. I can't be everywhere at once, and I don't want anyone getting lost or injured."

We all nod like we're supposed to and then peel off, April and I trailing after Cam, Bianca and Manu, who's telling a story that's making them both laugh. I glance sideways at April, who is gazing around with a smile on her face.

Walking up the slope, we head across a cool suspension bridge. We're halfway across when Manu starts jumping, making the whole thing sway and rock. I scream and snatch the railing, while April goes stiff beside me.

"Manu, stop!" Bianca tells him off while I scowl at him.

He gives us a sheepish grin, but then he's laughing again, jumping off the other end of the bridge and landing on the pathway beside Deek and Terry.

On shaky legs, I continue across the bridge, April and I walking quietly beside each other. One thing I love about April is that when we're hanging out like this, we don't have to talk. There's never awkward silence. We're just together, and there's no obligation to fill the space with anything. I really appreciate that about her. With Heath, it's never this quiet, but the thing I love about him is that he never expects me to say anything. He's happy just to talk about what's going on in his life.

There's something so golden about silence that so many people just don't get.

But April does.

I nudge her with my arm and grin. She smiles back at me, and my mind starts buzzing with ways to make her truly happy. How am I going to get her and Manu to interact this weekend?

We get to another bridge, and this time I wait until Manu is off the other end before even getting onto it. With the threat of him gone, I actually stop in the middle, gazing down the stream and instantly captured by the beauty of this place. It's so calm and peaceful here—the flowing river, the patches of blue sky between the puffy white clouds. The sun glistens off the water and—

"Come on, guys!" Cam's waiting for us so we know which way to turn, and we hurry up, following him down to a cave that is pitch black.

"What's that?" My voice hitches.

"The tunnel." Terry grins. "Grab your torches."

Cam hands me one from his bag, and I fumble it before passing it on to April and then taking another one.

I'm not a huge fan of the dark, and this tunnel is freaking me out a little. Why did I agree to come on this hike again? I don't remember them saying it was a long, narrow, completely pitch-black tunnel we were walking through! They just said tunnel. They made it sound like it was this safe, easy thing.

"You okay?" Bianca asks someone.

It takes me a second to realize she's talking to me.

I force a smile, too embarrassed to admit that I'm afraid of the dark. I'm nearly sixteen! I shouldn't be this scared.

"Yeah, I'm fine." Clamping my teeth against the frantic breaths wanting to punch out of me, I nod and keep my smile in place until Bianca looks away from me.

"If you stop about halfway through and turn your light off, you'll see some glowworms," Deek tells us.

"Awesome." April grins, passing me in the line.

I nearly snatch her hand and beg her not to leave me, but she's moved ahead in her excitement and I'm now at the back. My legs are kind of twitchy as I trail after the group. Just before I reach the opening, Manu glances at me, then stops and lets me go ahead of him.

"Why?" I narrow my eyes. "Are you going to play a trick on me?"

His face bunches like I've just offended him and he tuts. "No. You look scared. If I go behind you, you'll have torchlight in front and back."

I blink, totally taken aback by such a sweet gesture. I

should really be clarifying that I'm not scared, but the words won't come.

He raises his eyebrows and points at the tunnel with his torch. "Go."

Swallowing, I step into the dark entrance, the cold enveloping me immediately.

"You don't like the dark, or is it small spaces that freak you out?" Manu murmurs.

I want to tell him to stop talking about it, but his voice is actually kind of comforting in this weird way. The drips of water echoing off the cold stone are creepy. This is one of those times when talking is probably a good thing.

"Um." I lick my lip and admit, "Not a huge fan of the dark."

He snickers behind me. "I had a night-light until I was thirteen, but don't tell no one."

I smile and whisper, "I won't."

This weird sensation curls in my stomach, and I rub my hand over the warm fuzz, focusing on the beam of light in front of me. Dodging big muddy puddles, we slowly make our way through the tunnel, even enduring a small stint of utter darkness so we can check out the glowworms.

April loves that part.

I hold my breath while Manu stands behind me. I can feel him right there, and for some reason it stops me from fully freaking out. I imagine him huddled up in his bed when he was a kid, probably hugging some kind of teddy bear while he stared at the night-light on his wall. That's what I used to do anyway. It was my lighthouse across the stormy dark sea of carpet, and I'd stare at it until my eyes slipped closed.

I wonder if Manu was the same.

"Let's keep moving. Nearly there." Deek moves forward, and I see the circle of light at the end of the dark tunnel.

I want to focus on it, let it guide me to safety, but I also don't want to ass over, so I have to keep looking down at where I'm stepping.

It takes forever, but finally we burst into the light and my muscles uncoil instantly. Mr. Hamilton was right about it being a beautiful spot. To my right is this small waterfall, which cascades into a large swimming hole. It's not actually a hole, more like a blip in the river where the land forms a large circle the water can run through. It's a slow-moving current, though.

"We always jump off that rock in the summer." Cam points across the pool.

Bianca grins at him. "I would never have the guts to do that."

"Yeah you would." He smiles down at her. "You could hold my hand."

She laughs and I shudder. "It'd be so freezing right now."

"I'd do it." Manu laughs. "I'm gunna do it."

I spin and frown at him. "You're crazy. It's way too cold."

Terry laughs. "Go on, mate. Do the winter plunge."

Manu's already stripping off his clothes. I bulge my eyes and quickly spin away. April glances at me, fighting not to laugh. I'm glad she's enjoying this so much.

Manu's going to get hypothermia just so we can all have a laugh. This is ridiculous!

Running across the rocks in nothing but his red-and-black plaid boxers, Manu lets out a war cry, beats his chest a couple of times and plunges into the water.

I gasp and slap a hand over my mouth while everyone else cheers. Except April. She's laughing, her eyes dancing with pleasure as she watches Manu get out of the water. He's already shivering, but he's grinning like an idiot.

Crazy.

He's completely insane.

"Do some push-ups like Bear to warm up, mate." Cam chuckles, dropping down to do them with him.

I roll my eyes while the two guys compete to see who can do the most.

"Bear Grylls. I love that show," April murmurs, smiling as she watches on.

Oh yeah, she's got the hots for warrior boy over there.

I definitely need to make this happen for them.

It's time to get crazy Moo and sensible April together. They'll probably be a perfect match for each other.

23

STACEY

A fun game of touch has started up between Tane, Harper, Oscar and Mike. Even Beck's joined in, plus Mr. Hamilton and his other mate who didn't feel like going on the hike.

Maybe I should have gone on the hike, but I don't know. Something held me back.

I stand on the edge of our camping circle, wondering if I should run over and join in the game of touch rugby. It'd be a nice distraction.

"Hey." Hayden approaches, snapping a twig as he steps up next to me.

I jump in fright and turn to face him.

His forehead wrinkles with this sad kind of frown, and my stomach clenches. Are we about to talk? Is this it? The big chat we've been avoiding?

"What do you want to do now?" Hayden murmurs.

I'm not exactly sure what he means by that loaded question, so I take the chicken's way out and point at the game. "I was thinking of joining. You want to play too?"

Hayden's expression flatlines.

"What?"

"Nothing." He shakes his head.

"I always hate it when people do that." I turn to face him. "It's obviously something, so what is it?"

"No, it's fine. I was going to ask if you wanted to explore the area with me, so we could talk about the fact that we're just friends… or nothing."

I swallow, hating the hurt look on his face.

"But you go play with Mr. Yum. I know that's what you want to do."

"That isn't why I was going to play."

"Sure." Hayden nods.

I sigh and look to the ground, hating this feeling inside of me. Why does this have to be so difficult? "You know, you could play with us."

"And embarrass myself, and probably you, in the process?"

"You're not bad at sports. What are you talking about?"

"I saw your face when we were playing soccer with those kids. At Hamilton Gardens? Remember? You looked embarrassed."

My mouth goes dry, an image of his playful victory dance spinning through my brain. It was actually kind of cute, but that expression the older boy was making just—

"I see your face, Stacey. I know, okay? We've had this conversation already, and I don't want to get into a fight about it."

"It wasn't a conversation," I mutter. "You just yelled at me and then walked off."

"Well, it's not like you were butting in with any kind of counter. All I said was the truth, and you couldn't refute it because it's exactly how you feel, right? You just proved it when you introduced me as your and Bianca's friend. You don't want me as your boyfriend. Just say it!"

I bite my lips together, annoyed that I can't find my voice. Where's it gone? I used to be so ace at conflict; now I just stand there like a mute with no brain.

"Stacey? Are we just friends or not?" He raises his eyebrows, looking pissed and also a touch desperate.

I open my mouth, then close it, my insides writhing.

"Stacey?"

Great. Now he's getting impatient, and he obviously won't settle for the shrug I'm trying to give him.

"What does that even mean?" he snaps, mimicking me with an exaggerated shrug.

"I don't know!" I snap back. "I don't know, okay? I'm confused right now. I like you. Spending time with you is fun, but—"

"You just don't want to do it in public," he interrupts me with something I wasn't even going to say, but he's so set on believing it.

I mean, maybe yeah. I don't want to date him in public right now, but not for the reasons he thinks.

So why can't I just say that?

Instead, I barely whisper, "I'm not ready for everyone to know we're a couple."

"We're obviously not a couple. You've made that perfectly clear." He spins on his heel and stalks away from the campsite.

"Hayden, wait."

"Don't follow me!" he practically snarls. "Just give me some time to think. Go play. Go flirt. Do whatever the hell you want to do. I'm going for a walk. By myself!"

He stalks off and I watch him go, feeling like total crap.

24

WILLOW

M anu's now dressed, shoving his dry clothes straight over the top of his wet body. Honestly. I don't get him at all.

April and I found a perch on a fallen tree, the wood beneath us smooth and free of bark. The sun beats down on our little spot, warming our skin and getting me all excited for the summer. It's still a few months away, but there's only one term of school left to go, and then we're all free.

I'm going to have to think of some excuses for seeing Heath after ballet classes finish for the year. Hopefully April can help. Hopefully she'll be so loved up with Manu that she'll *want* to help me.

"Let's head back, ay, guys?" Terry beckons us back to the dark tunnel, and I take a torch from Cam when he passes it to me.

Hovering near the entrance, I notice Manu waiting like he did last time and figure now is a good moment to get something started.

April steps in ahead of me, and I indicate for Manu to go next.

"You sure?"

"Yeah. I've done it once now. I'm feeling okay about it." My jittery stomach is kind of telling me I'm full of it, but I try to ignore the feeling. This is for a good cause.

Manu eyes me for a moment, like he's not quite buying my lie. So I divert his attention, pointing into the dark tunnel. "Hey, you've met April, right?"

He looks at me like I'm weird. I guess he was introduced when we were loading up the cars this morning.

"She's Year 11, same as me."

"That's nice." Manu tips his head and turns like he wants to get away from this conversation.

"Hey, April! Wait up!" I call past him.

He stops and glances back at me. "If you want to walk with her, then you should go ahead of me."

"No, that's okay. You... uh, you walk with her. I'll follow you guys."

"You coming?" April shines her torch beam back at us. I

give her a cheesy smile and try to push Moo in that direction, but he's way more solid than I thought he'd be, like a deep-rooted tree that barely sways in the wind.

"Would you just go, please?" I give him a frustrated scowl. Why isn't he walking after April like I want him to?

A dark tunnel. That could be romantic, right? They could accidentally bump into each other. He could stop her from falling. Catch her against him.

I can picture it all now.

"Isn't she *your* friend?" he mutters, turning into the tunnel. "Didn't you bring her here so *you* could hang out with her?"

"Of course I did," I snip.

"Bet your fulla loved that. He probably wanted to come too. Where the hell is he?"

The hairs at the nape of my neck prickle, panic pinching as I pray his voice doesn't bounce off the rocks and right into Bianca's ears. "That's a stupid question when I've already told you I don't want my family knowing," I whisper-bark, then add in a lie for good measure. "Besides, he has to work. Can we stop talking about this, please?"

Manu tuts and walks forward, his beat-up sneaker slipping off a wet rock and into a puddle. "Aw, stink one."

He flicks out his shoe, and I try not to laugh. The way he talks is really funny sometimes.

I clear my throat, flicking my torch beam down the tunnel and noticing that April is way ahead of us.

Seriously?

I asked her to wait.

Maybe this is a good thing, though. I can plant a seed without her hearing me.

"Hey, Moo?"

"Yeah?" He rests his hand against the cold rock to balance himself.

"April's pretty, right? You should go have a conversation."

He goes still, his leg spread across a puddle as he turns to frown at me. "What are you up to?"

"Nothing. I just… She's a really nice person. You should get to know her."

"Not interested."

"Why not? She's kind, sweet, funny, *really* intelligent."

"Would you stop trying to sell me on some chick? I can find one on my own. Don't need your help." I shine the light in his face, and he gives me a withering look. "Based on the quality of your fulla, I think I'm safer without your advice."

I gasp. "What the hell is that supposed to mean?"

"You know."

I flick my torch beam away from his expression, not liking the look in his amber eyes. He doesn't know shit about me or Heath or anything.

With an irritated huff, I muscle past him. "You are so annoying!" I slip on a rock and end up bashing my shoulder on a sharp bit. It freaking hurts, and I can't help a little gasp of pain.

"You right?"

He reaches for me, but I push his hand away, leaning in close so I can whisper, "April likes you, okay? She thinks you're hot, and all you can do is stand there telling me I have bad taste in guys? You don't know anything about him."

"And she don't know anything about me. Neither do you, so why you trying to set us up?"

"I'm trying to be helpful."

"No, you're meddling. It'd just be easier for you if April had a boyfriend, wouldn't it? Then you wouldn't feel so bad every time you ditch her or use her to hang out with Mr. Secret. That's what happens, right? She's your best excuse."

I stumble away from him, my foot splashing into its own puddle. Freezing cold, muddy liquid instantly drenches my sock, but still I stand there glaring at him.

How the hell did he figure that out?

Manu narrows his eyes at me and lets out a scathing chuckle. "I'm right. Poor April. Who'd want a friend like you?"

"Shut up! You're an… an idiot. A… a… a stupid prick." My voice is trembling. My whole body is! "I wouldn't want her with you anyway. She needs to be with a guy who has more than two brain cells, not some dumbass like you."

Where are these words coming from?

I've never been this mean to anyone before.

An instant apology is pushing its way up my throat, but then Manu tips his head and gives me the finger. I shine my light beam over it, then huff and return the favor before storming off with a growl. I'm not apologizing to him!

My wet sock squelches as I try to stomp away, but puddles and slippery rocks slow me down, not to mention the suffocating darkness. I focus on my torch beam and keep plunging through the tunnel until I make it out the other side, my insides vibrating with outrage.

Manu just saw straight through me.

No one ever does that.

The only person I could never tell a lie to was Dad.

But not anymore.

Manu eases out of the tunnel. I glance over my shoulder to look at him, but his eyes dart quickly away, and he brushes past me to get to Cam and Bianca.

I guess I'll just have to stick with my original plan and avoid Manu at all costs this weekend. I wish he'd never been invited on this damn camping trip!

25

STACEY

The touch rugby game is over, and everyone has returned from their exploration. Willow seems in a particularly bad mood.

"You okay?" I ask her as she stomps past me.

"My sock got wet!"

Yikes! The world's about to end.

I refrain from teasing her and share a quick look with Harper instead. She's fighting a grin and winks at me.

It's nice seeing her a little more relaxed. She can be kind of uptight at home—playing the mother figure without actually being the mum. It must be hard to get that balance right.

I check my white watch, brushing my thumb over the digital screen and trying to figure out how long Hayden's been gone for. Playing touch with the others after he stomped off was kind of hard. I couldn't really concentrate and kept dropping the ball or passing it to the opposing team. Everyone started hassling me about it, and I tried to be good-natured instead of grumpy, but it was getting harder and harder. All I could picture was Hayden stalking away from me and telling me not to follow him.

Man, he was pissed.

He probably never wants to see me again.

That thought really hurts, like way more than I ever expected it to.

I've ruined it—whatever *it* was—and I don't know if we can ever make it right again. The idea of never hanging out with Hayden in his awesome bedroom or talking hair, fashion, house designs, watching *Project Runway*, going to concerts with him… it's a hot dagger straight through my chest.

Glancing at the track he disappeared down, I wonder which way he went. Surely he'll get over his huff and be back soon, but then what? Will he ignore me?

I can't let that happen.

I can't let this be the end.

When he returns, I really need to talk to him. Maybe we can go sit by the river and have a chat. I still don't know what I'm going to say. I like him. I miss hanging out with him. I want to go back to what we had. Maybe that's what we both need to do.

But a small part of me rebels against that idea. Kissing Hayden, although impulsive, was kind of fun. I liked it… like a lot.

He has great lips.

My mouth twitches as I finally capture the clear memory I've been chasing—the one outside the farmhouse with the stars twinkling above us and the night air crisp against our faces. His lips were so warm and soft and—

I let out an agonized sigh.

So why isn't *us* working?

Ever since we've tried to become a couple, it's been one mishap after another.

How do we have both? The friendship and the romance.

I just—

"You guys have fun?" Beck distracts me as he takes a seat in a camping chair beside me, directing his question to Cam and Bianca.

"Yeah, it was great." Bianca starts telling us how Manu went for a winter dip, and a quick banter kicks up between everyone. Manu takes it all with an easy grin before excusing himself to go and get changed.

"Just hang your wet stuff behind the tent. I've strung up a line." Beck points over his shoulder before doing a quick head count. "We're missing someone."

"Yeah, Hayden went for a walk," I murmur.

"When?"

"A while ago." I scratch my chin.

"He didn't tell me." Beck frowns.

Oh crap. That look on Beck's face.

Jumping to my feet, I put on an easy smile, not wanting Hayden to get in trouble with the grizzly bear. It was my fault he stormed off.

"I'll go find him. I know which way he went." I point over my shoulder as I walk backward, then spin and jump between two tents, taking off before anyone can ask me why Hayden would wander off alone and if I really do know which way he went, because I kind of don't.

"Can we go fishing now?" I hear Oscar distracting Beck for me, and I pick up my pace, pleased he won't be following me for a proper interrogation.

I shouldn't have just let Hayden storm off.

He's mad because I can't find my words. Maybe I should tell him that. Maybe talking to him, even if I have to stumble and let my words wander in a million different directions, will help me figure out what I need.

I mean, I don't really love the idea of doing that, but…

"Just find him," I mutter. "Maybe when you see him, the words will magically appear in your mouth."

Doubtful, but what else am I supposed to do? People are going to start noticing the tension between us if we don't sort this out, and if I can't explain myself to Hayden, how the hell am I supposed to do it with Beck or Tane or Harper or anyone else who's with us this weekend?

Striding up the hill, I stop at the top and do a slow one-eighty, trying to figure out which way Hayden might have gone.

"Having fun?" I glance to my right and notice Mr. Hella—I mean, Mr. Hamilton ambling toward me.

He has a towel draped over his shoulder, and his hair is kind of wet. Did he do a winter dip too? Crazy man.

And how is he not freezing, standing there in nothing but a T-shirt and cargo shorts? I glance at his impressive biceps and quickly avert my gaze. I'm about to find Hayden and have deep chats; I don't want to be thinking about this hottie while I'm doing it.

"It's Stacey, right?"

"Yeah." I smile, then point at his hair and clothing. "Aren't you freezing?"

He laughs. "Couldn't resist a little dip. It was frigid but refreshing."

"So, you are crazy, then."

He laughs again. It's a deep sound that travels right through me. "That's me. Anything for a rush."

"Ah, an extreme sportsman?"

"I like anything fast. Motorsport is what I love the most. You ever watch it?"

I shake my head, struggling to think of anything more boring than watching cars whizzing repeatedly around a track. They sound like mosquitoes—my least favorite bug. Actually, I don't really like any bugs, but mosquitoes have got to be the worst!

"I go to as many events as I can." Mr. Hamilton's still talking, throwing in a bunch of car names I don't recognize. "Love seeing those beauties race around a track."

Boring!

"You should come sometime. Feel the rush."

I give him a polite smile, having zero intention. I can think of a million other things I'd rather do. Like sit on Hayden's bed watching rom coms, or flick through fashion magazines with him and discuss pros and cons. I'd rather talk hair, movies, music.

"So, V-8s are probably my biggest passion."

I stare at Mr. Hamilton, his words turning to white noise as my mind throbs with this revelation that's hitting me so hard I'd be the world's biggest dork not to notice it.

Memories gush through me—Hayden's beautiful hands dancing through the air those times he dramatically retells stories from his childhood, the husky tone of his voice when he talks about his mum, his sweet look of concentration as he works with my hair like it's spun gold, that rapt look on his face when I'm telling him what I think about… well, anything.

Hayden, I whisper in my head, my heart starting to glow, yearn, pulse for him.

I blink, suddenly seeing Mr. Hamilton again and noticing something I never have before. He might be tall and strong and sexy, but he doesn't interest me at all.

Motorsports?

Are you kidding me?

I want Hayden. I want all of him, from his delicate hands to his beautiful eyes to his slender arms and tender kisses. I want his laughter and his amazing flamboyance. I *want* all that stuff, because it's interesting and funny, and I don't ever switch off when I'm talking to him because he always has something incredible to say. Time disappears when we're together. Being with him is what I love most, and I've been getting all confused when it's really so simple.

If I had to be stuck in a room with any human on the planet, I'd want it to be Hayden.

Holy crap!

I've got to find him. Like right now.

He needs to know that. He needs to know exactly how much he means to me.

"So, my friends have just taken a few drinks down to the river. You want to join?"

"Huh?" My nose wrinkles.

He just grins at me. "For a drink. Do you want to come have a drink with me?"

"Um… I'm a student. Should you really be inviting me to do that?"

"I don't teach you." He winks, and I take a step away when he leans forward a little.

He's flirting with me.

The student teacher is flirting with me.

What. The. Hell!

A flash of Jonas and his smooth smile annihilates me, and I'm suddenly slapped in the face by another blinding revelation.

Guys are pricks!

But not all guys.

Not Hayden.

A smile lights my face as I point past Mr. Hamilton's shoulder. "Actually, I'm just going this way."

"Alone?"

That better not be hope I hear in his voice!

I give him a steely glare, suddenly finding him way less attractive than I did before, and mutter, "Someone's waiting for me."

"Oh." And then his eyebrows rise. "Oh! A little secret rendezvous, huh?"

I force a smile, not loving the suggestive look on his face.

"Well, you be careful. It'll be dark soon."

I slip past him, ignoring the shiver that runs through me when his hand accidentally brushes mine.

You know what, he may be attractive, but only physically.

That's it.

I've been taking all this crap as signs, but the truth is... I *want* Hayden!

I'm suddenly desperate to find him, picking up my

pace and breaking into a light jog across the suspension bridge. I have no idea which direction he's gone, but I've got to find him.

Like now.

"Hayden!" I shout, jumping off the end of the bridge and hoping with everything inside of me that I find him soon, because finally I know what I want to say.

26

WILLOW

I watch Beck and the younger boys traipse off with their fishing gear.

They won't be too long, as Beck wants to be back with enough light left to set up the lanterns, prepare any fish they may have caught, and get dinner on the go.

Hopefully it'll be fresh fish and not sausages. I guess we'll just have to wait and see.

I managed to unearth a dry pair of socks from my pack. Everything is now sprawled across the tent floor, and I rush to shove it back in before tying on a pair of dry sneakers and heading back out to find April.

Tugging down my sweater, I rearrange it over my cargo pants and scan the middle camping area. She's not sitting with the others, who are now engaged in a game of cards.

Harper's hiding a giggle behind her hand while Tane grunts and picks up from the pile. He looks at the card and groans as Cam teases him.

"I should play poker with you, bro. You're like an open book." He chuckles while Tane lightly smacks him in the arm.

Turning away, I wave a little bug out of my face and move to the back of the tents. Manu is draping his wet clothes over the makeshift line, and April is standing next to him. I can't hear what she's saying and wonder if I should leave them to it. Maybe they don't need my help to get together.

After all Manu's bitching in the tunnel.

Seriously. What guy wouldn't want April? She's sweet and kind and cute.

Sure, she's shy and maybe a little awkward, but she'd be a catch.

What are they saying to each other?

Curiosity gets the better of me, and I stealthily inch within hearing range only to discover that I should have walked away.

Manu narrows his eyes, giving April a suspicious look. "I know what you girls are tryna do. No offense, but I'm just not into it."

April looks confused. "What are you talking about?"

"I know you think I'm hot, but you don't know me, and I don't know you either. I didn't come camping to hook up. I just want to hang out with my mates, all right?"

"Hook up?" April's forehead wrinkles as she tucks a loose lock of hair behind her ear, then brushes a little gnat off her face.

"Willow told me you like me."

April flushes bright red, her eyes turning to saucers. But then she spots me standing by the tent and they narrow into thin, angry slits. I swallow and wish I could disappear, but her eyes are like tractor beams, pulling me in. "Why did you say that to him?"

Manu whips around and sees me standing there.

"I... Well, I..." I flick my hair over my shoulder and point to Manu. "You told me he was hot, and I was just—"

"Trying to set us up?" April almost looks hurt by this as she crosses her arms and shrinks in on herself. "Why would you do that?"

"I-I thought you liked him." I wave a bug away from me and try for a smile that says *Please understand. I was trying to be nice.*

But April's mouth just drops open, obviously mortified by me saying it out loud like this.

Manu tuts and throws April a sympathetic look. "Basically she wants you out of the way so she can date that guy and not feel bad about it."

"I never said that!" I snap, my foot breaking a dry stick in half as I step forward to defend myself.

"But it's the truth, isn't it?" April's voice has a bitter edge to it. "He always has to come first. He's been that way his whole life. And now he's taking you away from me too!" Her eyes start to well with tears. "I knew this was going to happen. I told you to stay away, but you wouldn't listen, and now you're trying to set me up with some guy just to ease your conscience!"

"That's not what I'm— I mean, I'm—"

April mutters something dark under her breath and storms off before I can even finish my sentence. As soon as she's out of sight, I grab Manu's shirtsleeve and force him to turn around and face me.

"Why did you do that?" I slap his arm.

It obviously has zero effect, except to maybe piss him off a little. His amber eyes darken a shade, but I don't shy away from him. I'm too annoyed.

So we stand there glaring at each other until he tuts and mutters, "I'm just being honest. Maybe you should try it."

"I hate you," I seethe. "Stop ruining everything!"

I push past him, my legs wobbling a little as I jump around guy ropes and try to find April.

Why did Manu say that to her?

Doesn't he understand that lying can be the kinder option?

What's so great about the truth anyway? It only gets people hurt!

27

HAYDEN

So it's getting late. I can tell by the drop in temperature and the slight fade of the sun. It's not dark or anything yet, but the day will soon turn, and I'm seriously screwed.

Turns out storming off in a rage and not keeping track of where you're walking is not a great idea.

Turns out that jumping off the trail because you don't want to be spotted by a group walking your direction is an even worse idea.

I ran up the embankment, putting as much distance as I could between myself and strangers, then just kept walking. Tears were blurring my vision as I bashed branches and ferns out of my way.

Then I just slumped down in a puddle of my own misery and bathed in a deep pool of self-pity.

Eventually my muscles started to ache, and the numb disappointment was turning into an itch of realization. I couldn't spend the night in the bush feeling sorry for myself. Whether I wanted to or not, I had to face Stacey again.

She doesn't want me. She's made that clear.

I somehow have to let go of this awesome thing we had going.

"Should never have kissed her," I mutter to myself as I spin in a circle again.

The sad fact is it might not even be an issue.

Looking up at the surrounding trees, I feel them towering over me, easing in to make this vast forest feel like a prison cell. The endless green ocean of bush I'm standing in only reminds me that I am one hundred percent lost, and I have no idea which direction I should be going.

My dad would tell me off for leaving the compass in my backpack, which is safely tucked away in my tent. But even if I did have a compass, it wouldn't do me much good because I don't know which direction I stormed away from.

We set everything up around the middle of the day. The sun was high in the sky, and I have no idea if the camp-site is east, west, north or south of my current location.

I wasn't paying attention.

I don't even know if I turned left or right when I jumped off the end of that suspension bridge. The river was to my right, I guess, so I can go by that, but I can't see or hear the river right now.

"Totally screwed," I mutter, clumping down the slope until I reach a wall of impenetrable bush.

With a sigh, I turn around and hike back up, shoving my way through the thick forest in the hopes of finding some kind of trail. Even a little one would do. Little trails tend to lead to bigger ones. And if I find a bigger one, I can probably find my way back.

"Before dark would be good, mate." I scoff and shake my head.

Dad would be so embarrassed if he knew what I'd done.

He'd get that pitying kind of frown on his face. His eyebrows would pucker with that slight confusion.

"I don't understand how you work, Hayden. "

"I don't know what to do with you."

Mum was the only one who got me.

For a moment there, I thought Stacey did too, but it turns out that only works in a platonic way.

I'm not boyfriend material.

I'm not son material.

I'm just… ugh!

"I don't know what the hell I am!" I screech, my high voice bouncing back to me and making me cringe. I clear my throat and try to lower it. "I don't know what I am."

With a tut, I roll my eyes. I sound like a moron when I talk that way. And it hurts my throat.

"Face it," I murmur. "You're a lost cause."

I get why Stacey doesn't want me.

In this moment, *I* don't even want me.

Why couldn't I just be more like my brothers? More like Cam or Tane or even Manu?

Why'd I have to be born this way?

Why doesn't society celebrate guys like me? I've got qualities too; they're just not the ones people look for when they're creating their dream date.

I'm the guy you run to when you're getting ready for your dream date. The one girls bare their souls to while you apply makeup and do their hair.

I'm that guy.

And there's nothing wrong with that guy.

Yet somehow there is.

Mum would call bullshit on that statement, but she's

not here right now. She's not here ever again. I've got no one in my corner anymore.

My throat swells with this ache that makes it hurt to swallow.

"I miss you," I whisper, fresh tears getting the better of me.

Wiping a dirty hand across my eyes, I try to brush them away, then quickly give up. Why am I bothering? I'm in the middle of freaking nowhere all by myself. I don't have to try and be anything other than me right now.

And me would bawl my eyes out, because I'm lost in more ways than I'd like to be.

No mum.

No girlfriend.

Just a pathetic boy in the woods.

28

WILLOW

I find April by the river. She's sitting on a boulder, her feet dangling over the edge as she swipes tears off her face.

I'm still pissed at Manu for saying that stuff to her.

What the hell is wrong with him?

As soon as I reach April's side, I rest my hand on her shoulder and softly say, "Don't listen to what he said. Moo's full of shit."

April glances at me with a sad smile, shrugging me off her. "No he's not. You are."

She may as well have slapped me in the face. My eyes start to burn as I cross my arms and think about walking away from her.

But it's April.

My friend.

I need her on my side.

In spite of the fact that I'd rather hear anything else right now, Manu's advice to be honest is plaguing me. Is he right? Should I just fess up?

Maybe I was in the wrong to meddle. I mean, I was only trying to help. I really do want April to be happy, but I guess I had an ulterior motive as well. If I think about it that way, what I did was kind of mean.

I've never been a mean person before. What's going on with me right now?

I don't like it.

Tentatively perching next to April, I pick up a large pebble and start rubbing my thumb over its smooth surface. "I'm sorry." My voice wobbles. "I thought I was doing a good thing by trying to set you up. You said he was hot."

"Yeah. Hot. That's it. I didn't say I wanted to get with him. I simply said he was better-looking than that student teacher everyone's drooling over."

"*I'm* not drooling over him," I murmur softly.

April snickers and shakes her head. "I'm not ready for a boyfriend, or any kind of relationship. I like being single. I just want a friend." She turns to face me. "You. I want you to be my friend."

I blink, surprised by the uncertainty in her voice. "I'll always be your friend."

April looks like she doesn't believe me. "It's not the same. When we first met, we clicked and we hung out heaps and it was great. But then my brother had to come and ruin everything. He always has to be the center of the universe."

I swallow. The look on April's face is so painful, like she's in agony or wounded or something. Reaching for her hand, I curl my fingers into hers.

"I didn't mean to fall in love with him. It just happened."

"How? Why?" Her pitching voice and wrinkled expression confuse me.

Isn't it obvious? Heath is handsome and dynamic and—

"What do you mean?" I tip my head.

"Why do you love him? He's such a two-faced asshole."

"Not with me." A flash of him getting pissy with me the other day makes me pause to swallow, but then I remind myself of the chocolates. His sweet words. The fact that he needs me. "He loves me. He…" I want to say he makes me feel safe, but that's not quite right. How do I explain myself?

Throwing the pebble into the water, I listen to the plop and then it disappears. Collecting up another one, I

237

chew the inside of my cheek and start to murmur, "He's different to anyone I've ever met. He makes me *feel* again."

April's eyebrows flicker, and she's gazing at me like she's never seen me this way before.

Maybe she hasn't.

I lick my lips and draw out the truth, its spiky nettles hurting my throat and tongue as I start to talk. "When Mum and Dad died, I just... I shut down. I couldn't talk. There were no words to explain what I was feeling. Everything was foggy and cold. All the time. I felt like I was dead but still breathing. Trapped in this prison of... I don't know." I shake my head, hating how hard it is to explain myself. "But then I met you, and I started to feel a little bit better, and then Heath came along and he... he made me feel alive again. He's exciting and a little bit dangerous or forbidden or something. I don't know what it is, but it makes me *feel*. I'm feeling again, and it's... it's... liberating." My voice is starting to quiver like I'm fighting tears, but my eyes are dry.

April squeezes my hand, her smile and eyes so sad. "I don't want you to get hurt."

"He won't hurt me." For some reason, I can't look her in the eye when I say that, so I duck my head and press on with the truth. "He needs me. We need each other. It's love."

April doesn't say anything, and I look up to check on her.

She bites her lips together, her thumb rubbing the back of my hand. "He's not the only one who loves you. Your family. Your friends." She points at her chest. "We love you too. We want you to be happy."

"But I am." My voice pitches. My smile feels too tight.

I don't know why. I'm in the truth zone right now. Aren't I?

"We want you to be safe."

My smile falters.

Safe.

What is it with that word? That feeling.

The last time I felt truly safe, Dad was alive. It was Christmas Day, and he was listening to me harp on about my amazing grand jeté that I managed to pull off at the Christmas concert. I was thriving off his smile, that beam of pride in his eyes. I can see his face so clearly. Then he asked me to dance for him. My favorite part of the recital. So, I jumped up and spun around the living room to Christmas music while everyone else was busy in the kitchen getting ready for lunch. I added in a few of my own moves, letting the music flow through me like water. There was no ballet teacher there to correct my position. I could just... dance. It didn't matter what move I did, I knew without a doubt that

Dad would love it. He wouldn't judge it or tell me where to improve; he was just enjoying watching his daughter dance. Loving me no matter what mistakes I made.

I was safe in his company. And now I'll never have it again.

An immense pain fills my chest, and I dig my fingers into the gap between my breasts. It hurts! It really hurts! I have to think of something else or I'm going to go insane.

Heath's hands on me. Heath covering me. Pulling me into a world of excitement. Bringing me back to life.

I start to breathe again, relatively normally.

April's hand is on my back now. She's rubbing between my shoulders, looking all concerned.

"I'm okay," I whisper. "I'm okay."

April still doesn't believe me, but she's nice enough to smile and softly say, "Thanks for telling me the truth. I didn't know about that whole foggy, cold prison thing."

I stare at the flowing water, ambling along like it's taking a stroll. I like the sound of it. Peaceful and soothing in a way. Like it can't be touched by pain.

"I've never told anyone that before," I whisper.

"Thanks for telling *me*." April looks kind of honored when I glance at her face. Her smile grows a little wider, although it still looks uncertain. "And if Heath is helping you, then great. I just… I feel like he's changing you too, and I don't want to lose my friend."

"You won't lose me," I quickly reassure her. "And I promise to not set you up with idiots again."

April giggles. "Manu's not an idiot. At least I don't think he is."

"I'm not so sure." I put on a joking voice, which makes her laugh again, and the tight strings inside of me start to unravel.

The pain in my chest is easing, and I can take a full breath without feeling like I'm going to throw up.

"Should we head back?" April asks.

"Soon." I squeeze her hand. "Let's skim rocks for a while. The most jumps wins a chocolate bar."

"Ooo. You're on, sista." April jumps up and starts sorting through the pebbles at our feet, looking for the flat ones.

I do the same as the late afternoon sunlight turns the trees golden across the water.

I gaze at its stunning beam, a weird sensation stirring through me. It's kind of like a warm fuzziness that I don't mind so much.

29

STACEY

S o, I turned right at the end of the second bridge, and all I can hope is that it was the better move. Should I have gone left instead?

What compelled me to go right?

I'd love to think there was some cosmic connection between Hayden and me. Like somehow in my subconscious, I know which way he went and that's what prompted me to turn right after the bridge, but what the hell do I know?

After the week we've had, we're so *not* connected that he's probably on the other side of the river.

A shaky sigh whistles between my lips, worry gnawing on my stomach.

It's been ages.

I feel like I've been walking forever, and I still haven't found him.

As the light grows slowly dimmer, I start to question when I should be turning back. Beck will be annoyed if I don't check in, but how do I return without Hayden?

Maybe he's already back at the camp, and now everyone will be wondering where I am.

I plant my feet, assessing the ever-thickening bush around me and wondering what to do. This trail is narrowing to a skinny end, and soon I'll be clambering through thick forest and undergrowth.

"Hayden!" I shout. "Hayden, please! If you can hear me, please come out!"

The only response is the twitter of a couple of birds. Wings flap and something whooshes past me, making me shudder.

It's eerie in this isolated spot. The resonating sounds of nature feel big and frightening.

I should turn around and head back.

But Hayden.

I need to find him.

What if he's lost out here? Hurt. Wounded.

It's all my fault.

I shouldn't have let him believe for a microsecond that he wasn't good enough for me.

He is.

He's better than me.

He's everything.

And now that I can't find him, I'm feeling it more deeply than ever.

What if I never see him again?

The thought is brutal enough to buckle me and I bend over, bracing my hands on my knees as fear swamps me.

"Hayden!" I cry out again, tears starting to punch through my breaths.

I have to find him.

I need him.

I think I might even love him.

"HAYDEN!"

30

WILLOW

I'm feeling pretty good as April and I amble back to the campsite. Twilight is setting in, and although I don't love the darkness, it will feel kind of magical sitting in our tent circle with the lanterns going. Kind of like that bonfire at the beginning of this year when we all decided to stay on the farm.

I couldn't go back to Wellington. The very thought of it punched the words out of my chest, the first words I'd spoken since Mum and Dad died.

Now look at me, baring all to April.

The counselor Harper's forcing me to see has been trying for months to get me to talk about my feelings, my parents, all that stuff, and I haven't budged. I've stubbornly sat in that chair for the designated hour and given her the bare minimum, sometimes even nothing at all.

But tonight.

With April, I… just blurted it out.

It's weird that I'm feeling so good.

Even thinking about Mum and Dad hurts. Talking is even worse, but I did and it didn't kill me.

"Smells like fresh fish." April sniffs the air and I join her, my smile growing.

The boys must have had some luck at the river.

Hustling forward, we follow the delicious scent until we reach the cooker. Beck is moving beautiful white fillets of fish around in a fry pan, adding just a touch of salt.

"It'll just be a taste each, but we've got loaves of bread and lots of spread."

"Sausages too, if we want to cook those up afterward." Harper grins. "This can be like a fish entree before we kick into the oh-so-classy sausage-in-bread main course."

Tane laughs. "Sounds awesome. What's for dessert?" He wiggles his eyebrows at her and… is she blushing?

Why does she do that around Tane?

It's like she likes him or something, but there's no way. He's so not her type. She wants a guy like Dylan—all city and sophistication, elegance, class. I'm guessing they'll get back together when he returns from his overseas trip. Although I don't want to think about it too much. Will that mean Harper moves back to Wellington next year?

I bite the inside of my cheek and study Tane. He's a rugged country boy through and through. I mean, look at him. He's standing there in a checkered Swanndri and shorts, thick woolen socks and big tramping boots with a beanie on his head. He couldn't be more bushman if he tried.

I take a seat on the picnic blanket next to my sister. April joins me, crossing her legs and shivering.

"I might go get my jacket." She rubs her arms. "The temperature is definitely dropping."

"Yeah, good call. Can you grab mine? It's the green one near the top of my pack."

"Sweet." She jumps up and goes to grab our jackets while Bianca pops her head out of the tent.

"You're back?" Her voice rises with relief until she spots me and starts to frown. "Are Stacey and Hayden with you?"

"No." I shake my head. "April and I were just down by the river."

Manu pops out of his tent and looks at me. I catch his gaze for just a second before averting my eyes to the picnic rug. Why do I suddenly feel hot?

This scalding sensation that I don't like burns my shoulders and neck.

It's impossible to look at him, not when I was so nasty. Not when maybe he was just a little bit right about the whole truth thing. But that still didn't mean he had to dump me in it and say that stuff to hurt April's feelings.

I might feel kind of guilty over what I said to him, but I'm also mad at him.

"Wait a second, what did you just say?" Beck looks up from the cooker. "Are they still not back yet?" He flicks off the gas and stands up. "Where the hell did they go?"

"Stacey took off that way." Oscar points behind him.

"It's getting dark. I told them they had to be back by now."

"Stacey left ages ago."

Beck's forehead wrinkles as he runs a hand through his hair. "Shit! How did I not notice! Too distracted by these bloody fish."

"Could we call them?" I jump up, hating it when Beck gets agitated like this. He can be a little scary with his loud voice. I head to my tent for the phone before I remember that—

"There's no reception out here." Beck spins and shouts across to Mr. Hamilton and his crew. "You lot seen Stacey or Hayden?"

"What's the matter?" April whispers to me as she hands me my jacket.

I pull it on and murmur, "Stacey and Hayden aren't back yet."

Mr. Hamilton strolls over. "Sorry, what was that?"

"Missing a couple of kids. Stacey and Hayden. You seen 'em?"

"Oh. Uh." He looks around, his eyebrows wrinkling in confusion as he obviously scans heads. "I saw Stacey. She said she was meeting someone."

"Where?" Beck snaps.

Mr. Hamilton points behind him. "She was crossing the bridge."

"When?"

"About an hour ago. Maybe a little more?"

Beck huffs and points to the cooker. "Cover the fish with a tea towel or something, Oz. We better go look for these guys before it gets dark."

"They could be anywhere." Cam pulls his sweater on. "The trails lead off all over the place."

"Did you see which direction she went after the bridge?" Beck asks Mr. Hamilton.

"No. I figured she knew where she was going."

"But Hayden wasn't with her?"

"She was on her own, but said she was meeting someone."

"Why would they go sneaking off?" Beck throws his arms up.

Bianca and Cam share a quick look, and I start to wonder if Stacey and Hayden are more than just friends. That's weird. I didn't think Hayden would be Stacey's type.

Beck scrubs a hand down his face. "All right. This is what we're gunna do. I want us all to split into groups of two and three. Fan out, taking different trails. You're to walk for exactly thirty minutes, and if you haven't found them in that time, you turn right back around and come here to check in."

"I'll get Terry and Deek to stick around here, if you like. Tell them to stay put if they do come back before the hour's up," Mr. Hamilton suggests. "Karl and I will help you with the search."

"Good idea. We should be able to find them if we spread out." Beck keeps stroking his beard, and I can't help picking up his worried vibe. It filters into me, curling my stomach and making me jittery.

31

HAYDEN

It's going to be dark soon. I check my watch and have to actually light the screen to see the time.

Yep. Within the next half hour, the sun will have set and I'll be completely lost in a dark forest.

The idea makes my legs give out, and I slump to the ground, landing on a sharp rock.

"Ouch!" I spit out a few curses, hating my predicament and idiocy.

I just had to storm off.

I just had to be dramatic about it.

With an irritated huff, I lift my knees to my chest and perch my forehead against my arms.

Aw, man. If I could turn back time.

What would I do differently?

"Maybe not yell at the girl I care so much about?" I wrinkle my nose. "Maybe tell her that she doesn't need some buff bloke when she could have me."

My eyes start to burn.

"What, you mean the crybaby?" My own voice mocks me, and I slap my leg, sitting back with a scowl. "No! I mean the guy who could treat her the way she deserves. The guy who'd listen to her and make her smile and treat her like a queen! That guy! I can be that guy, and I should have frickin' told her that instead of getting all pissy about the fact that she's attracted to some student teacher! Arggh!!" I slap my legs a few more times, frustration coursing through me.

I'm so busy beating myself up that I nearly miss the faint cry.

"Hayden!"

I go still, my eyebrows popping high.

"Was that…?" I whisper.

"Hay-den!"

I gasp and scramble to my feet, straining to hear which direction the call came from.

"Hayden!"

"Stacey?" I shout and start running down the hill, veering slightly to my right. "Stace!"

"Hayden!"

I think she might have heard me. Her voice pitched at the end.

Yes! She found me!

Gravity helps me pick up speed and I'm soon coursing down the hill, crashing through bushes to get to her. I get bashed in the face a couple of times and nearly lose my footing once, but I manage to regain my balance before assing forward onto my face. I catch myself against a tree, whacking my shoulder but not letting the pain slow me down.

My body is stinging with cuts and grazes as I fight nature in order to get to Stacey.

"Hayden, where are you?" she shouts.

"I'm here! I'm coming!"

Her voice is getting louder. We must be closing in on each other. Do I hear thumping feet too? Is she running to find me?

My heart skips with glee until a pained scream makes it jolt to a stop.

"Stacey!" I leap over a fern and nearly break my ankle, falling the last meter down the embankment until I land on a barely-there path in time to see Stacey tumbling down the slope below me. "Stace!"

I launch after her, landing painfully on the hard ground

but managing to grab the back of her jacket. But her downward momentum is too strong, and we're now both sliding down a steep, muddy slope.

Stacey screams again and I tighten my grip, grappling to hold onto something that will stop our fall. Everything I snatch runs straight through my hands, and I let out a cry of desperation when I see a whole lot of nothing screaming toward us.

"No, no, no!" I shout, shoving out my leg and managing to hook my hiking boot around a narrow tree trunk.

My left hand snatches a fallen branch that seems to hold, and I feel like my right arm is being wrenched out of its socket as Stace tumbles over the edge and I'm stretched from my two anchor points.

"Oh shit, oh shit, oh shit!" Stacey's crying.

"It's okay. I've got you."

I'm in so much pain right now it's hard to talk, but I am *not* letting her go.

Stacey's panting as she swings, and I can feel my grasp on her jacket loosening.

"I don't want to drop you!" I shout.

She pivots and snatches my arm, her fingers digging into me as she scrambles to climb up the slippery face.

"Ahh!" she screams and then whimpers. "I think I've busted my ankle."

"I've got you," I grit out, the pain radiating through my body warning me that it won't be for long. Even so, I punch out a quick breath and promise her, "I won't let go. So just climb up on your good foot. Let's do this."

She grips my arm and does this kind of hopping movement to pull herself a little higher. It's an effort, but she manages to grab the edge of the ridge and then snatches the shoulder of my jacket.

Clenching my teeth, I swallow the cry of agony as little by little, grunt by grunt, she hauls her body up to safety. As soon as only her legs are dangling, I let go of her jacket and grab the waistband of her pants, using the little strength I have left to drag her up until her feet are clear of the edge.

Finally letting go of the branch, I roll my aching body onto its back and lie there panting. Stacey whimpers beside me, and I know I should reach for her, somehow comfort her, but I can't move for a second.

Black dots are spotting my vision.

Everything hurts.

My chest is radiating pain, and my arm has its own heartbeat.

A dry scraping of leaves and loose sticks makes me turn my head. Stacey is working her way closer. She crawls up, whimpering and crying until she can rest her head on my chest.

It hurts, but I can't tell her that right now.

I just need to feel her lying beside me.

To know she's safe.

"You just saved my life," she whispers.

I smile weakly up to the darkening sky but can't say anything.

She moves to get a better look at my face, and I can't stifle my hiss.

"Are you hurt?" She touches a scratch on my cheek, which is the least painful thing right now.

"I've felt better," I manage, lightly patting her hand.

Her face bunches, and then she lets out a sob, resting her forehead against my chest. I cup the back of her head because I don't know what else to do. It hurts to move, and I don't have any words to make this better.

Images of her falling have my insides quaking.

"I lost you," Stacey whimpers against my muddy jacket. Suddenly her head jolts up, her blue eyes vibrant with tears. "I don't ever want to lose you again. I'm sorry," she whispers, wiping snot and tears off her face. "I'm so sorry."

I slide my hand around to her cheek, wiping the tears

with my thumb and still struggling to form words past the haze of pain.

I want to tell her it's all right.

I want to murmur that she's so incredibly beautiful right now.

But I don't get the chance, because she launches for my mouth, her quivering lips pressing against mine.

It actually kind of hurts, but like hell I'm doing anything other than kissing her back.

She found me.

We're together.

It doesn't even matter what state we're in right now.

We're just… together.

32

WILLOW

T he air is taut and suffocating as we stand around for our final instructions.

I can tell we're all trying not to worry, but something has just snapped, and we all *are* worried. Like big-time.

I can't even think about the idea of Stacey and Hayden disappearing for good.

Stacey is cool. I don't want to lose her.

This family can't take any more.

We have to stick together.

Mates for life!

Panic courses through me in nauseating waves, and I sway just a little on my feet.

April steadies me with her arm. "Are you okay?"

"Yeah." I swallow and force a smile. "Just missing Heath," I whisper back.

It's mostly true. I'd feel so much better if he were with me right now. He's strong and brave and determined. He'd hold me close and grab my hand, pulling me into the bush to find Stacey and Hayden. He wouldn't let anything get in his way. He'd—

Beck claps his hands to get our attention. "Right. One group's going to head across the bridge and turn left. Cam and Bee, you went that way before. You take that path."

"I can go that way too," April says.

I step forward to stand beside her while Beck gives her a tight smile, then points at the boys. "I'll take you two with me and we'll take the right trail off the bridge. Justin, why don't you come that way too? I'm pretty sure the trail forks about two kilometers in, and we can split there." Mr. Hamilton nods. "Tane, Harp, they may have gotten themselves turned around, so you head north up the river. And, ah... Manu and... Willow." He points at me. "You head south."

"But I should go—" I try to interrupt him, but he totally ignores me, talking over the top of my protest.

"I want everyone searching for no more than an hour. It'll be totally dark by then, and I want you all back here. Remember, thirty minutes one way and then you head back. If we haven't found them by then, I'll drive out of here until I find reception and call the police. They can get search and rescue involved." Beck rubs a hand over his mouth, looking a little sick. "Everyone know what they have to do?"

I raise my hand. "I'm gunna go with April."

"I don't want Manu going on his own."

"So pair him with someone else, then?" I keep my eyes off Moo, just in case he's giving me the evils or something, but come on. Beck can't expect me to go with him. I mean, I told him to his face that I hated him. I'm surprised Manu isn't kicking up a big stink as well.

"We don't have time for this, Will," Harper clips. "Just go with Moo."

She grabs a torch and heads off with Tane, while Bee, Cam and April start for the bridge.

"April!" I spread my arms wide, shouting to her back.

She spins around, her torch beam waving over me. "Just go with Manu. I'll see you soon."

I can't believe she's doing this to me!

We just made up again, and now she's shitting all over my massive peace offering. Abandoning me and leaving me with Manu. Of all the people to be stuck with!

"You coming?" He passes me a torch and I snatch it off

him with a huff, flicking it on and keeping my eyes on the beam as I trudge after him.

I know I should be thinking about Stacey and Hayden right now, but it's going to be hard looking for them when I'm stuck with the last person on the planet I want to be with.

Closing my eyes for a second, I think about Heath, wishing he would magically materialize to take me away from all this. We could speed off in his sexy car to some secluded spot. Thank God this camping thing will all be over soon and I can be back in his arms. Back in his car with a bottle in my hand or hidden away in some secret grove where it's just us.

No words.

No emotions.

Just him and me.

33

STACEY

The forest floor is hard and cold. There's an evening dampness seeping up from the earth, and I'm starting to feel it through my jacket. Now that we've recovered from the shock, my senses are coming back on line properly, and there's one message it's blasting loud and clear—we need to get moving. We need to get back to the campsite.

I shiver and Hayden pulls me closer, rubbing my back to try and warm me up.

"You're shaking."

"It's c-cold. We need to get back to camp. If we j-just head straight up, d-do you think we'll find the trail?"

Hayden swivels his head to look up the hill. "Yeah, probably. Can't believe I was so close to it. I didn't even realize. I got myself totally turned around."

"Never leave th-the trail, right? Even I-I know that."

He snickers. "I was upset. You don't think straight when you're fighting tears and big emotions."

Guilt swamps me. If my teeth weren't chattering, I'd make more of an effort to find those words again, the ones I wanted to tell him after talking to Mr. Motorsports. Maybe when we're warm and dry, back at camp with my fingers curled around a hot chocolate, I'll be able to bare my soul.

I just really need to get warm.

Moving slowly, I push myself up, resting my hand on Hayden's chest until he lets out a stifled cry.

"What's the matter?"

"Maybe I broke a rib or two. I don't know." His hand is shaking as he cradles his side. "Everything's pretty sore right now." He goes to sit up and lets out another cry of pain, reaching for his right shoulder.

"You're a mess." I let out a watery laugh. "You did that s-saving me, didn't you?"

Hayden closes his eyes with a sigh. "Stace, I would have busted my entire body for you." His lips twitch with a smile. "I think I might have, actually."

I rise to my knees and then struggle to my feet, attempting to rest some weight on my throbbing ankle.

As soon as the toe of my sneaker touches the ground, fire courses through my foot and I stumble forward.

"Ow," I whimper as Hayden reaches out to catch me, then whimpers himself.

I flop back to my knees and scrape my fingers through my hair. Bits of dirt and debris are clinging to my wayward curls. I pluck out a little and flick it off my fingers.

Hayden's eyes glimmer with kind of a smile. "We're both a mess right now."

Another watery laughs pops out of me, and I touch his face. "What are we gunna do?"

It's hard to talk with the pain and chilly shudders rippling through me.

Hayden struggles up to one elbow and looks up the hill again. "Aw, man. It looks like a really long way from here."

"I know," I whimper, desperation surging through me. With a busted foot or ankle or whatever the hell is up with me, and Hayden basically a wreck, we're screwed.

"I guess we need to put our Bear Grylls hats on."

"Our what?" I sniff.

"Please tell me you've heard of Bear. My dad idolizes the guy."

My teeth chatter as I try to smile at him. "Yeah, I've h-heard of him. That army guy wh-who likes to put his life on the line all the t-time. The survi-vi-val one."

Hayden snickers and rubs my arm again, but it obviously hurts. "That's him. If he were here, he'd be telling us that we need to get warm and find ourselves some shelter away from this wind. Think you've got the strength to drag your ass up toward that clump of bushes?"

I look up the hill and think I see the clump he's talking about. "Yeah."

"Let's go." Hayden grunts and starts using his legs to propel himself up the hill. I start crawling and we wriggle our way up, side by side, helping each other where we can. Once we reach the clump of bush, we kind of work our way around it and then into it.

It's an effort, but finally we manage to find a little shelter from the chilly wind and lean against the base of a solid pine tree. We're panting pretty hard, but the exertion did me good, got my blood pumping a little. It's not until my heart is beating regularly again that the chills come back, weakening my jaw and making my teeth chatter.

"Here." Hayden parts his legs and unzips his jacket, encouraging me to lean against him.

"But what about your ribs?"

"We need the warmth."

He's right, but… "Maybe you should lean against me. The only thing that hurts on my body is my foot."

"Just get in here." He gives me a pointed look, gently coaxing me to lie against him. He hisses when my weight presses into him, then adjusts my position so I'm on his left side.

"Are you okay?" I whisper, not fully able to relax.

He presses down on my shoulder, forcing me to rest against him, and swings his good arm around my body. "Yeah, I'm fine."

"Liar," I murmur against his collarbone.

He snickers and tugs his jacket so it's kind of coming around my body too. I tug the other half to try and form a bit of a barrier around us. Between the undergrowth and each other, I'm slowly starting to warm up a little.

Hayden rests his cheek against the top of my head. "They'll find us soon. It's basically dark, and there's no way Beck won't be worried."

"And annoyed," I murmur.

"Probably more worried. I guess we should be grateful we're injured. They can't be too pissed off when they find us."

I let out yet another watery laugh.

"We've come camping with a bunch of people who care enough to search through the night. Don't worry, Stace. We'll be okay. You found me, so they'll find us."

"But we can't just stay here all night."

"We can last the night. In the morning, we'll be able to see everything clearly. We'll have had some rest, and then we can figure out the next step."

I shudder and rest my forehead into the crook of his neck.

"But they'll find us before then. It'll be okay."

It'll be okay.

People say that a lot, usually when everything is very much *not* okay. But I don't know, when Hayden says it, I find myself believing him.

Closing my eyes, that sense of fear that wants to envelop me eases a little. Hayden's arm is secure around my body. It makes me realize that if I'm going to be stuck in the bush with anyone right now, I'm glad it's him.

34

WILLOW

I t feels like we've been out here for hours, but it's only been fifteen minutes. With an irritated tut, I negotiate the unstable rocks we're trying to traverse as we head south along the river.

Why did Stacey and Hayden have to go off anyway?

I should be sitting around eating hot fish right now.

It's hard not to be slightly frustrated with them, and it's impossible not to be ticked off by this situation.

I still don't get why April just took off and left me with Manu. It's a betrayal. That's the way it feels anyway. Maybe she's getting me back for trying to set her up with Manu. I didn't think she was that vindictive, but there you go.

You think you know a person…

"You right?" Manu flicks his torch back to check on me.

"Fine," I mutter, shining my beam back on him.

For a guy who I thought was stupid, he's doing a really bad job of proving it. He seems more than competent out here. Why is that bugging me?

I glance up, annoyed by my own confusion. There's still a touch of light in the sky, but it's that really deep blue now. It'll be all black soon, and then we'll be negotiating these rocks with nothing but torch beams.

"Should we head back?" I flinch at a noise on my right. I don't know what the hell that was, but I don't like it.

I pick up my pace, leaping over a few stones to catch up with Manu.

I might not like the guy, but he's the only one around right now.

"Nah. We'll give it ten more minutes, then turn back, ay?"

"All right."

"Hayden! Stace!" Manu shouts, swinging his light around to highlight the other side of the river. He's been calling out every now and then, and I haven't bothered to join in. His voice is way louder than mine.

He stops and takes a minute to investigate a patch of darkness.

"What is it?" I whisper, my heart picking up pace.

"Thought I saw something, but…" He shrugs. "Nothin'."

"They probably didn't even come this way," I murmur.

"Yeah, but Beck's covering all the bases. We'd feel pretty stink if we didn't check down here and that's where they were."

"True," I mutter and move after him, jumping onto an unstable rock that turns on me.

My ankle twists and I yell, flinging my arms out.

Manu spins back, catching my elbow to steady me. His grip is light and reassuring. Not like Heath's grip, which is always so strong.

Why am I comparing?

"You okay?"

"Yeah, the rock just moved."

Wriggling my arm free, I rub the place he was touching me. There's this tingle under my clothing. I have no idea why. Manu has long, thick fingers, and there's obvious strength there, but his touch was so light just now.

What is with that tingle?

I rub my arm a little harder as Manu turns back to the search.

"Hayden! Stace!" Manu shouts again, then tuts and

shakes his head. "It'll be real dark soon. Hope we can find 'em before Beck has to call the police."

"They're going to be okay, right?" I suddenly blurt the question, this sharp sensation pulsing through my body.

Manu stops walking and turns to look at me. His lips twitch with a half smile. "Yeah. They'll be right. We'll find 'em."

I swallow, the sound thick and audible.

"Come on." He holds out his hand, obviously waiting for me to take it.

I gaze at his open palm and don't move.

"It was only to steady you." He shrugs and starts walking again. "You probably don't really need it, though, right? You're a ballerina, ay? Harper told me. Bet you got great balance and all that. Can you stand on your toe tips or do any of those twirly things? Stuff in the air?"

I don't really like talking about ballet very much, but "twirly things" and "toe tips" is kind of cute. My lips curl at the corners in spite of my effort.

"Yeah, I can do a few things," I softly murmur, wondering if I *can* actually do any of that stuff anymore. I haven't been en pointe since before Christmas. All those things I spent hours working toward, all the training… have I lost it?

It doesn't matter, I suppose. I rub my belly and remind myself that I never have to dance again, so *it doesn't matter* what I can and can't do anymore.

Unnerved by this spiky sensation on my shoulders, I march behind Manu. The anger that was fueling me before sparks up again, and I cling to it. Anger hurts less than spikes and doesn't confuse me the way tingles do.

This is good.

I'm annoyed because it's dark and kind of scary out here and Manu totally dumped me in it with April. Although, that kind of led to a good conversation in the end, but still! He was a jerk.

Sucking in a breath, I flick my torch around as Manu shouts out names again. The dark yellow beam highlights the trees to my right. I can't see anything, but a rustling in the leaves freaks me out, so I swing the torch over the water and completely miss the big rock that catches my foot and flings me forward.

I land with a hard smack, the torch bumping out of my hand. Its beam shines straight up and I gaze at the light, struggling to breathe. There's this sharp, blinding pain in my shin right now, and it freaking hurts.

It hurts so much.

Manu crouches down beside me. "You right?"

I open my mouth, but no sound will come out. My

hands are shaking as I spin onto my butt and reach for my shin. I want to touch it, squeeze it, anything to take the pain away, but I also don't want to make it worse.

Resting his torch on the ground, Manu uses a couple of rocks to hold it steady and angles the beam at my leg. I glance down, hissing when I notice the line of blood soaking into my pants. I must have cracked my shin on a rock. It's too dark to tell which one, but I'm cursing it all the same. I'll curse all these rocks!

I just want the pain to go away.

Being a dancer, I've always been extra cautious to make sure I never broke or twisted anything. I'd work hard at ballet, pushing my body to the limit, but that was in a controlled environment. Bleeding toes and aching muscles are nothing compared to slicing your shin on a rock.

Stupid nature. I don't even want to be out here.

"Hmmm. Ouch," Manu murmurs as he reaches for my leg. He suddenly stops and looks up at me. "Is it okay if I touch you?"

I'm too surprised by the question to do anything other than blink.

"Just so I can take a proper look. I won't if you don't want me to."

What is going on right now? Why is my heart hammering? He's asking permission to touch me. Heath's never done that.

Why am I comparing again?

I squeeze my eyes shut, confusion making it hard to think straight.

"It looks pretty sore. Do you want me to see if I can fix it? Or I can take you back to camp, if you'd be more comfortable there."

I open my eyes and gaze at him. I can't see the intricacies of his amber eyes in this dim light, but the expression on his face is so patient and undemanding.

What is going on right now?

Where did idiot Moo go? The guy who was a jerk? The one I was mad at?

Glancing away from his sweet expression, I whisper, "You can look."

My hands tremble as he passes me the torch.

"Just shine it right there."

I point it on my leg as he gently rolls up my pants to check the damage.

The movement hurts, but I try not to complain as he pulls the material away from the wound, exposing an ugly gash with instant bruising already forming around it.

Manu hisses. "No muscle to take the blow. No wonder it hurts so much. Your bone probably feels dented."

I bite my lips together. Looking at that blood is making me feel nauseous.

"Not hurting you, am I?"

He strikes me dumb with the question.

No. He's not hurting me. His hand is gently cradling my calf muscle, his long thumb warm against my skin.

I shake my head. It's all I can manage.

"Could need stitches. I don't know, but we better wrap it, ay?"

I nod and he looks around, then purses his lips and starts shrugging out of his jacket and sweater.

"What are you doing?"

"Making a bandage." He grins, looking kind of proud as he whips off his T-shirt.

"Won't you be cold?"

"I'll be right," he murmurs as goose bumps ripple his taut skin. His body is lean but chiseled. You can tell he's an athlete. I can't stop staring at his smooth brown skin as he rips up his T-shirt and starts winding the makeshift bandage around my leg.

His touch is delicate and sweet. And confusing.

I didn't expect this from him.

He's Moo, for crying out loud—the reckless idiot who is always running late and making a joke out of everything.

I'm getting that warm feeling again, but I don't know why.

Part of me wants to embrace it, curl into its heat and just relish the happy sensation, but another part of me is warned away.

I have Heath.

He makes me warm.

No, he makes me something else.

Alive, I guess.

He makes me alive, not warm or tingling.

Which is a good thing... right?

35

STACEY

I t's hard not to conjure the inevitable as we lie here in the darkness.

It's only getting colder.

Seriously. Camping in the winter. What kind of crazy-ass idea is that anyway?

We're going to freeze out here.

I'm gunna turn into an ice cube, and I'll never see Bianca again. I'll die without the chance to say goodbye or make anything right.

It'll be quick, just like it was with Mum and Dad.

One minute I'm there, and the next I'm gone.

If I'd known it was the last time I was going to see my parents, I wouldn't have been so flippant with my goodbye. I would have given Dad the biggest hug and held tight for ages. I would have told Mum how wonderful she is and how much I love her.

I can't even remember the last thing I said to either of them.

"I'm sorry," I whisper.

"What?"

Hayden's murmur makes me jump, but then I go still. This is my chance. I'm right here in Hayden's arms. This is my chance to make it right.

Come on, words, don't fail me this time!

"I'm sorry I, um…" Tears start to choke me. "I'm sorry if I made you feel like I didn't want you or… the whole being a couple in public thing. I just…" I sniff and go quiet, not sure how to voice any of the things floating in my head. I'm usually so good at saying exactly what I think. I've lost that, and I miss it. And I need it back, like right now!

"Stace." Hayden sighs, his chest deflating beneath me. "What do you want? I'll be whatever you need me to be. I just hate the way things have been this week. I miss you. I miss us."

"Me too," I whisper.

"Things just got so screwed up, and I didn't know why it was happening, and I got scared and… and I shouldn't have yelled at you at school and gotten so snotty and defensive. It just hurt that you didn't want to be with me. I was jealous of Mr. Hamilton, and feeling like I wasn't good enough for you. That's a pretty sucky truth to face."

"But you are good enough."

"I'm not everything you want, and I have to accept that. I don't want to lose you, but—"

"I don't want to lose you either." I grip his arm.

"So, friends again?"

I go still, then shake my head. "No."

Hayden sucks in a breath like he's fighting tears. "Too hard, right? I never should have kissed you. I screwed up everything."

I spin to face him, and he hisses at the sudden movement.

"I'm sorry. I'm sorry." I rest my hand on his cheek, wishing I could see his eyes properly, but maybe it's easier that I can't. There are so many things buzzing inside of me and I think they all need to come out. "I… I've been feeling really lost, and, um… I didn't mean to hurt you. I've just been trying to figure out…" I huff. "You were my friend, like the best friend ever, and then you were more, and then our first date was pretty bad, and it felt like some kind of sign."

Hayden whines. "It was pretty bad. The cracking of heads was probably the defining moment for us."

I let out this weak laugh, but it gets choked off by the stuff I have to say. "Then Mr. Hamilton showed up, and I saw him and I was really attracted to him, and I took that as another sign. Like how could I be attracted to someone else when I was supposed to be your girl-friend?" I blink at tears, guilt scorching me. "And then you yelled at me, and I let you. I just stood there letting you make all these horrible assumptions about yourself that just aren't true." Tears get the better of me, spilling over my lashes. "And now we're injured and freezing to death in the bush. It's like since we crossed that line from friendship into romance, things have been working against us. Maybe the universe is saying we shouldn't be together this way, but I hate the thought of not being with you."

Hayden doesn't say anything, and I scramble to fill the space. "Thing is, the universe has kind of been a total asshole ever since Mum and Dad died. I tried to find a new me because I couldn't face a world without them. So I pretended like they weren't dead. I refused to deal with it and hooked up with Jonas as a way of distracting myself. And I got burned pretty bad."

"Yeah. Asshole," Hayden mutters, and I close my eyes, knowing I have to tell him.

"No, he like tied me to a stake and humiliated me beyond anything I've ever..." Sobs shake my belly, and

I can't speak for a moment, this high-pitched squeak coming out of my throat instead.

Hayden shifts, obviously trying to see my face, which I've tucked into the crook of his neck. "Stace?"

My lips tremble as I wrench the truth out of me. "He recorded us having sex and posted it online."

Hayden jerks but then goes still, like he's turned to stone.

Do I keep talking?

What's he thinking right now?

I have to make this better. I have to keep going.

My words speed up as I punch them out quickly. "After that, I just wanted to hide, but I couldn't. And then I found you. And you didn't know, and you'd lost your mum, so you understood that part of me. You helped me without even knowing it. You became the best friend I've ever had, and then you kissed me. And I wasn't sure what to think. I wanted it to be something, but then—"

"I'm sorry," Hayden whispers, his hand curling around my neck as he kisses the top of my head. "I'm so sorry Jonas did that to you. If I'd known…"

"I don't want it to affect me, but I can't shake this feeling that people are always watching me. I don't know who saw the video, but there are guys at school who have *definitely* seen it. They moan like they're horny every time I walk past them. I'm sure they've seen me naked. They've watched me lose my virginity." And the body-jerking sobs are back again.

Hayden squeezes me against him, pressing his lips into my head as he shakes too. "That's why you wanted to cut your hair. To change yourself."

I nod, struggling to inhale a full breath. "It didn't work the way I'd hoped. I'm still me. I'm still the girl in the video."

"No one can see it anymore, can they?"

"No. It's been taken offline, but…" I shake my head. "The damage has been done."

Hayden squeezes the back of my neck, his lips trembling when he kisses my forehead again. "I really despised him for hurting you, but now whatever a stronger word for hate is, it's that. I'm feeling that toward that asshole!"

Hayden's shout makes me flinch, but I rest back against him, a smile curving my lips up. "You've helped me so much. I didn't think I'd ever feel anything for a guy again, but then you kissed me."

Hayden's beautiful fingers find my face in the darkness, his thumb rubbing tears off my skin.

"I want to be with you," I whisper. "I love so many things about you, but I've been so confused." I suck in a ragged breath. "I don't know who I am right now. There's parts of the old me that I really miss—the sport, the fact that I was so good at speaking my mind, the energetic person I used to be. But Jonas, the type of guy I always fell for, stole my voice or my confidence or something." I swipe my finger under my nose and sniff. "I want to find that again, but I don't want to be who I used to be either. There's parts of the new me that feel pretty good, and I'm just… lost."

I whimper against Hayden's shoulder, and he kisses my hair again. I really love how he does that. "I care about you so much. You're so many good things. Things that are right for me. Things I never thought I'd fall for."

He doesn't say anything for a long time, and once my crying has dulled to a manageable whimper, his soft voice fills the night air. "You know, my mum always used to say that the whole 'finding yourself' thing was BS. I don't know if I agree with her one hundred percent, because we're all born the way we are. But she did use to say that you needed to figure out what you *want* to be and then become that person. Stace, you've been through this really shitty time and got served way more than anyone deserves, but you have a choice. I mean, we all have a choice, right? I've been making stupid decisions. I never should have stormed off. I should have stayed and made us talk it through like we're doing now. I was being a whiny baby, and that's not the guy I want to be." He sighs. "My point is, why don't you just take the parts of the old and the new that you like and squish them together?"

I've never thought about it that way, and the idea makes me smile. I shift my head back so I can gaze up at his shadowy face.

His fingers trace a line from my earlobe to my chin. "I would never hurt you the way Jonas did. I will always regret kissing you without asking your permission. I was just nervous, and I'd been crushing on you for so long. I saw a chance, and I went for it. But I didn't know about Jonas. All I know is that being with you makes me so happy. I love talking to you about all the stuff we're both into, listening to music with you, watching TV with you. That stuff is way more important than anything else to me. We don't have to kiss or get physical. I just want to be with you."

My heart's suddenly all warm and gooey. "I like being in your arms right now."

He chuckles. "I know they're not strong enough for you, but—"

"They are." I squeeze his elbow. "You stopped me from falling, in more ways than one." I smile. "I want us. I want you. I know you'd never burn me."

He sucks in a breath, blinking at tears. "I wouldn't. I may not be strong and buff like Mr. Hamilton, but Stace, I can love you and care for you and treat you the way you deserve. I'd be really good at that. If you let me, I'll be the best boyfriend you could ever wish for."

And I know it.

As I lean up to find his lips in the darkness, I know it with my whole heart.

Hayden isn't my type, at least the type I thought I wanted, but he's right for me.

He's the one.

Pressing my lips gently against his, I seek out the comfort of his tongue and find it immediately.

Man, he's a good kisser.

I don't know why I let all those stupid doubts get in the way, but I'm going to make sure they never do again.

36

WILLOW

My leg is strapped up, and the darkness has fully closed in. It's turning me into a jittery mess. Staring out at that black expanse is creepy. Even my torch beam seems to get swallowed up by it.

Manu's putting his clothes back on. As soon as he zips up his jacket, he takes the torch off me and scans the area. I scramble to retrieve my own, needing something to hold onto. Glancing to my left, the darkness feels like a monster that wants to take me out—a big black mouth roaring toward me.

I suck in a short breath to try and quell my racing heart.

"Thanks for your help," I snip, my voice like staccato.

"It's all right."

"Did your… dad teach you how to do that?" Talking is

making my nerves less fried. I need to hear a voice in this darkness or I'll lose my mind.

Manu crouches back down, shining the torch between us. "I don't got no dad. He, uh… was an older fulla, knocked Mum up in high school and then took off. Didn't want no part of it." He clenches his jaw, and I want to say I'm sorry that happened to her, but I can't find my voice. "It's been me and Mum mostly. We started out with her parents when I was a baby, but I don't know what happened. Think they was trying to raise me like I was their babe, and Mum wanted to do the job. She said they didn't think she could, and she was determined to prove them wrong. So, that's what she does. Works her butt off all the time to prove to everyone that she can do it. She don't take charity."

How do you feel about that? That's what the counselor would say.

I bite the inside of my cheek, hating that question.

"But I got it good." He pauses, his eyes darting to the rocks at our feet. "I…" He works his jaw to the side, then glances at me. "I didn't lose no one, you know? 'Cause I never knew my old man, so… it's not like… like you. Must hurt real bad what yous guys went through."

It's hard to breathe for a second, but eventually I manage to rasp, "Yeah."

"You miss 'em? Like all the time?"

I shake my head. "Not every second of every day. Just in moments. I never see it coming, but all of a sudden, a memory will just come to life in my head and haunt me. Or I'll be doing something random and just wish until it hurts that Dad was there to watch me or… Mum was telling me to stop texting my friends and get on with my homework." My voice has gone all squeaky. My eyes are burning. I can't see because of the tears.

I suck in a breath and blink the tears away. What is with me this weekend? I need to stop opening my mouth and blabbing all this stuff. It hurts!

"I always hate when my mum says that to me, but I know she only does 'cause she wants me to have a good life. She don't want me to be stupid."

I glance down at him, wishing I could tell him I was sorry for saying he was, but he's looking away from me, and then he stands.

The words I need don't reach my mouth.

"You think you can walk?"

"Huh?"

"We need to keep moving. Get back to camp. Beck wanted us to only be an hour. With your bung leg, we'll probably be late now, so we should get moving."

"But what about Stacey and Hayden?"

"We're no help to anyone if we get back to camp late.

That'll just stress Beck out, and he's probably worried enough as it is."

"Okay. Good point." I nod, happy to get out of the expansive darkness. The promised comfort of lanterns and a circle of tents force me to my feet.

But as soon as I rise, my throbbing leg shoots pain down to my toes and right up my thigh.

"Ahh." I gasp and Manu steadies me, his hand cradling my elbow to keep me upright. "It really hurts."

"I can help you if you want?"

I nod and he steps close, resting his hand around my waist and pulling my other arm over his shoulder. He's quite a bit taller than me, which makes it slightly awkward, but we stumble along together, me on tiptoes and him grunting at the awkward angle.

"This is tricky." He lets out a breathy laugh after ten or so steps. "Maybe I could carry you."

"Um…" My eyes dart into the darkness and then swing back to him. "Yeah. Okay." I swallow, feeling nervous as he gently picks me up and starts negotiating the rocks. It's a bumpy ride and obviously a bit of a struggle for him, but he's not complaining.

As he silently walks me to safety, I get that warm fuzzy feeling again. For some reason, me dancing in the living room on Christmas Day flashes through my mind. I blink away the memory and focus back on the feel of

Manu's body. My arm around his neck, the short breaths that puff out of him, the way his body moves with such ease. He's a born athlete.

And he's carrying me.

Even after I was so mean to him.

He gave me his shirt.

I close my eyes, guilt smashing into me like a battering ram. It feels awful.

"You're not a stupid idiot," I murmur when we finally reach the flatter ground and he starts walking for the tents. "You're not a prick. And I… I don't hate you."

He stops and gazes down at me. I shine the torch upward so I can see his face. He's looking at me like he's trying to figure me out.

Then the side of his mouth tips up in a half smile. "I'm used to people thinking I'm dumb."

"I shouldn't have called you any of that mean stuff. I'm sorry. I don't know why I said it."

"You were pissed at me for outing you. Which I probably shouldn't have done. It was kind of mean of me too. You know, dumping you in it like that with your friend. I just wanted you to be honest… with yourself, mostly. But it's not really my place. So… you know… I'm sorry."

I blink, fighting the urge to cry again.

"Did you sort it with April, or is she still mad?"

"She forgave me… I think." With a thick swallow, I give him a nervous glance and confess. "I told her the truth and, um… she liked that."

He snickers. "Took my advice, ay?"

"Yeah, well, you're not stupid, so… it was good advice." This makes him laugh his melodic laugh. It rises up and down, and I wait for it to settle back to silence before whispering, "Thank you for looking after me tonight."

"Just trying to do the right thing. Don't always pull it off, but maybe I did all right tonight." He hitches me in his arms, and I'm aware of just how long he's been carrying me.

"I can try walking again."

"Nah, I've gotchu."

"I just don't want you to hurt yourself because of me."

He makes this noise between a scoff and a hiss, then smiles down at me. "You're not that heavy, ballerina girl. I bench more than you at the gym."

He looks kind of proud of himself for this, and I grin, not saying anything when he hitches me again. He may bench more than me, but I bet he doesn't carry those weights all the way from the river to the campsite. He'll be relieved when he puts me down.

But will I?

That's a weird question, and totally unexpected.

But I've just got this sense that when he places me down at the campsite, those warm fuzzies are going to evaporate, and I'll feel cold again.

37

HAYDEN

If I'm gunna die, I want it to be this way, with the girl I love wrapped up in my arms.

It's true.

I love her.

I'm not going to tell her yet. I want to wait. I want us to have some good times together as a couple first. I want a decent date that isn't drenched in pressure and cock-ups.

I want us to get back to that cool place we were in before.

She needs to feel totally comfortable and safe before I pull out the L-word.

Having her open up tonight, tell me all of that stuff… I don't know, it just made me fall even harder. I can't believe Jonas did that to her. I'm not a violent guy, but I would cross that line for him. I hope I never see him, because I would no doubt get my ass kicked trying to make a point. I'd do it for her, though. Stacey's the kind of girl you risk your life for.

I'm so relieved she's into me.

She wants me because I'm her best friend and we're good together. Even if she is attracted to Mr. Hamilton, it's...

"You know what?" I whisper.

"What?"

"All those signs, the fact that you think Mr. Hamilton is hot, I wouldn't worry about those."

"Oh yeah? And why is that?" Stacey runs her finger along the neck of my sweater.

"Well, I have the total hots for Mae Whitman."

She goes still. "Who?"

"That actress from *The Duff*."

Stacey sits up, and I stifle my groan. "Sorry." I think she's wincing and potentially frowning. It's hard to make out her expression in the darkness. "Are you talking about the short, dark-haired one? The main character?"

"Yeah." I nod.

"You think she's hot?"

"Yes. I'm totally into her." I grin.

"But…" Stacey's jacket rustles as she shakes her head. "She doesn't look anything like me."

My smile grows a little bigger. "Exactly my point. I'm attracted to her, but that doesn't mean I want to be with her. I want to hang with you because you make me happy and you're fun to be around. Don't get me wrong, I think you are off-the-charts gorgeous, but that's not why I want you to be my girl."

She doesn't say anything, and I wish I had a torch right now. I want to see her face so badly.

She sniffs and lets out a short chuckle. "You always have the right words."

"Not always," I shake my head. "I suck when I'm pissed off. The drivel that comes out of me is pathetic, and when I'm scared, I… There are no words, not really. I just kind of fumble the alphabet."

Stacey giggles. "I'm pretty good when I'm angry. At least I used to be."

I reach for her, patting my way up her shoulder and neck until I can cradle her cheek. "You will be again. If that's something you want. Remember—it's up to you."

"Yeah." She lets out a contented sigh and leans back against me—slow and gentle. I wrap my good arm around her, snuggling her close.

She's still shaking a little. I hate that I can't warm her up more, but I seriously think trying to get out of here in the dark, with our injured bodies, is a stupid idea. As soon as it gets light, we can make a move. Hopefully by then my body won't hurt so bad.

Closing my eyes, I will sleep—or restoration, or something—to revitalize me.

Unfortunately, Dad's face pops into my mind. Man, he'll be disappointed in me. Getting lost and then injured. I'm already dreading our conversation.

"You okay?" Stacey runs her hand over my chest and tucks it around my waist.

"Yeah, just thinking about my dad."

"Will he be worried?"

"Probably more annoyed than worried."

"Why would he be?"

"I got lost. I didn't take any of the survival gear he insisted I bring. I stormed off in a huff, and now we're here."

Stacey tuts. "Well, you need to tell him that you saved my life."

I kiss the top of her head, a shudder running through me when I think about how close that was. To be honest, the fall probably wasn't big enough to kill her. Injure her, most definitely. But she could have tumbled straight into the river. That's the scary part. It could have swept her downstream, freezing her in the process.

I hold her a little tighter, even though it hurts me.

"You need to make him see Hayden."

I tip my head, waiting for her to explain what she means, but she doesn't say anything. "See Hayden. What does that mean?"

"Look, I don't know the whole story, I just get the feeling from everything you've told me that he's so busy trying to turn you into one of the boys that he's missing the whole point. You're not like your brothers, and that's a *good* thing. You should be proud that you're like your mum. And your dad should be too! You are an amazing person, Hayden Thorp, and you don't need to *man up*. What does that even mean anyway? It's basically implying that every guy who isn't sporty and strong and blokey isn't a man, which is bullshit! Some of the best men in the world are totally metrosexual, gay or effeminate. If all men were blokes, we wouldn't have half the amazing fashion or designer food or architecture or any of that stuff! So, next time you see your dad, you look him in the eye and tell him, 'I am amazing just the way I am. I may not be a bloke like you, but blokes like you need guys like me. Who the hell do you think designs the houses you build, huh?'"

I raise my eyebrows, my lips parting as I take in Stacey's epic spiel.

"Did you hear me?" she practically snaps.

I snicker and nod. "Yeah. I, um… You know what, Stace? I think you're getting your mojo back. That voice you're missing… I just heard it."

She giggles and sniffs again, a shudder running through her. I try to pull her against me even more, but we're kind of as close as we can possibly get right now.

I rub her back and arms, wondering how painful this night will be. I don't want her developing hypothermia, and the temperature will only drop lower the longer we're out here.

"It's okay." Her teeth chatter. "For a while there, I thought m-maybe we weren't going to make it, but now that you have to s-say that stuff to your dad, I'm pretty determined not to d-die."

"That's good." I chuckle and am about to crack another joke when I hear a faint call. I jerk, my head jolting up so fast I lightly smack the tree behind me. "What's that?"

"Sta-ce!"

She gasps and jerks up as well. "Here!" she screams. "We're down here!"

I holler with her, both of us shouting like maniacs. Our

volume only increases when we catch the beams of light swinging through the trees and hear the thumping of boots.

Relief washes through me in thick waves as two large shadows appear before us. When they crouch down to check us out, I'm a little gutted to see it's Mr. Hamilton.

Great.

I try not to let it bug me as he checks on Stacey, then lifts her into his arms when she says she can't walk.

The other guy bends down to help me up. I wince and hiss. "My shoulder."

"Dislocated?" he asks, wrapping his arm around my waist to steady me.

"Don't think so." I cradle my elbow. "Just knackered."

"Come on, I'll help you." He starts guiding me up the slippery hill, basically having to push me as my wobbly legs struggle and my head starts to spin. "We've been looking for you guys for ages. Beck's kind of frantic. He sent Tane up to the main road to call the police."

We make it to the track, Mr. Hamilton walking ahead. I watch Stacey's injured foot swinging back and forth.

"Hey, careful with my girlfriend, mate," I call, my insides pinching. Will Stacey mind me saying that?

Mr. Hamilton glances over his shoulder with a snicker. "Your girlfriend?"

"Yes," Stacey snaps. "His girlfriend. Do you have a problem with that?"

My lips twitch as Mr. Hamilton stammers out a reply. "No, no. It's all good."

The guy beside me chuckles and softly murmurs, "Score, mate."

"I know," I whisper, this immense joy bursting inside of me.

In spite of the agony I'm in, I shuffle back to the campground, supported by this big bloke of a guy and feeling like the king of the world.

38

WILLOW

"We found 'em! They're here!" someone starts shouting from the top of the rise.

Relief pounds through me, hope soaring high as Mr. Hamilton rushes down the hill with Stacey in his arms.

Beck jumps over the guy ropes, running to his side. Taking Stacey off him, he carries her into the main circle and gently places her down just as Tane arrives back.

"You found 'em!" He tips his head back. "Thank God! I'll head back up and let the police know it's all good."

He takes off running for the car again while Bianca nestles down next to her sister. "Are you okay? Are you hurt?"

She's been crying nonstop since she returned with Cam and April. Cam's been doing his best to comfort her, but what can you really say to make it better? Bianca was no doubt contemplating life without her sister.

That deathly thought was niggling at me too, making me ill.

Stacey's not my twin, but she's become like a cousin. We've already lost so much. We can't lose more. We just can't!

"It's okay. It's okay." Beck eases off Stacey's boot while she writhes in agony.

Hayden takes an awkward seat beside her, grimacing when he tips sideways and bangs against Cam.

"You right, mate?"

"Buggered shoulder," he murmurs, looking ghostly white. "How's Stacey's foot?"

"Ballooning," Beck mutters. I can't see his face, but I bet it's bunched with concern.

Cam cringes, his eyebrows popping high. Her ankle must be massive, which is a bad sign.

Harper twitches next to me, obviously wanting to go look but refusing to leave my side. The second I appeared in Manu's arms, she had a mini freak-out, thinking I'd broken my leg or something. She investigated the wound by lantern light and decided it probably didn't need stitches.

"I bet it hurts," she murmured.

"Yeah, it's throbbing."

"You may have to take a few days off ballet."

I stiffened and forced a smile. "I'll be okay. I'm sure it'll heal quickly."

She gave me a reluctant nod before re-bandaging the wound with proper stuff from the first aid kit. I doubt Manu's going to want his shredded, bloodstained T-shirt back, but I did offer to wash it for him.

He just grinned at me. "Nah, it's all good."

A smile tugs at my lips as I watch him sit down next to Hayden. Cam's doing most of the talking and questioning, but Manu's there, a quiet pillar keeping Hayden upright.

Poor guy looks like he might keel over at any moment.

He keeps throwing worried glances at Stacey. Now that her boot is off, she's crying.

"We got Panadol in that kit, right?" Beck glances over his shoulder, and Harper starts rustling through the first aid kit.

"We should probably bind it too." She finally leaves me, and it's hard to ignore the cold whiff of air that flows through the space she just created.

I shiver and hunch over, holding my elbows to keep myself warm.

"We need to get these guys to the hospital." Harper looks to Beck.

He nods and turns around, looking grim. "Everyone grab essentials only. We'll come back and pack up the site tomorrow."

"We can do that for ya." Mr. Hamilton's a little out of breath from carrying Stacey. Resting his hands on his hips, he looks all worried, gazing down at Stacey and then Hayden.

"Thanks, mate." Beck stands, shaking his hand and patting him on the shoulder. "Thanks so much for finding them. I was just about to head out again when you showed up."

"They were down an embankment."

"We fell," Stacey murmurs. "At least I did, and then Hayden caught me."

"What were you doing wandering off the trail anyway?" Beck scowls, his voice a little snappy. With his big beard and the eerie shadows across his face, he looks kind of scary. I hunch a little further into myself while Hayden and Stacey share a quick look.

Beck tuts, flicking his hand through the air. "Look, it doesn't matter right now. You're safe, but you're injured. Let's get you right, and then I can yell at you."

My lips twitch with a grin at the look on Hayden's face, but Stacey's fighting a smile. Beck may seem scary sometimes, but I think he's got a heart of gold underneath all that rugged gruffness. He's not my dad, not even close, but he does look after us. I'll give him that.

April perches beside me, her knee jiggling. "I'm so glad they're okay."

"Yeah." I nod.

"Right." Beck claps his hands. "As soon as Tane gets back, I want him to take Harper and the girls home. Bianca, you can come with me and the wounded. Cam and Manu, you're in charge of Ozzy and Mike. Head back to the farmhouse, and we'll return to deal with the camp stuff in the morning." He does a slow circle. "Everyone clear on what we're doing?"

"Yes." We all nod, obviously too tired or rattled to argue.

Not that we need to argue. It's a good plan.

We'll be safe at the farmhouse, and I guess it's better than staying here.

Manu walks past me to get something out of the tent while April tugs on my arm and encourages me to follow her. She supports my side while I hobble to our tent.

I should be glad we're heading home.

I'm grateful April's with me again, although I still want

to call her on the fact that she ditched me to search with Cam and Bianca.

"You got everything you need?"

I pull my cell phone out of my bag and nod, hobbling after her to wait for Tane in the carpark.

Harper jumps up beside me, threading her arm around my waist to support me.

"Thanks," I murmur, glancing over my shoulder to see Manu rounding up the boys.

Is it weird that I'm suddenly feeling fragile?

I don't get it. I'm driving home to safety, but the act of walking away from the guy who carried me is making me feel strange.

By the time we reach the hospital, I'm in agony. I'm warm, the adrenaline has worn off, and my ankle is throbbing. I'm trying not to complain, because Hayden looks green. His head is resting against the window, his eyes shut as he nurses his shoulder.

Bianca's in the front seat, finishing up her phone call with Hayden's dad.

"He'll be here soon." She hangs up and runs around to open my door for me.

"You help Hayden," Beck says to her. "I've got Stace."

Reaching into the car, he gently lifts me out and carries me into the emergency room. It's still kind of busy considering how late it is. Beck parks me in a chair, and Hayden flops down beside me, groaning while Beck walks up to the counter to get some immediate attention. Slumping down in his seat, Hayden rests his head on my shoulder and I lean my cheek against his, relief easing its way between the points of pain.

We go through the rigmarole of filling in forms—hospital, ACC, insurance. It's kind of endless, and Beck's getting more and more frustrated by it all.

"Here, let me." Bianca takes it off him and finishes the form while we wait for Hayden's dad to show.

He bustles in about twenty minutes later, looking slightly panicked when he spots his pale son. Hayden's head lifts off my shoulder and he sits up, looking kind of edgy as his dad rushes between the seats.

"You right, mate?"

"Yeah, Dad, I'm fabulous."

Plunking into a chair opposite his son, he lightly touches Hayden's knee, looking sick with worry. I try to smile at him, but my lips aren't working properly. Everything hurts.

Thankfully, a doctor shows up, calling me first, but I ask if Hayden can be seen instead.

"I think his injuries are worse than mine."

"No way." Hayden shakes his head. "You go."

"Hayden." I give him a pointed look. "Broken ribs, remember?"

"Broken ankle," he argues back.

I frown at him.

"Hayden Thorp," a doctor calls into the waiting room, killing our argument before it can really begin. We both struggle to our feet, Hayden's dad supporting him while Beck picks me up again and walks me through to an emergency cubicle.

After rehashing my story to the doctor and then being poked and prodded, I'm sent down for X-rays.

It takes forever, and I'm seriously over everything by the time I'm sent back upstairs to wait for the results.

The nurse props my foot up on a stack of pillows, gently draping a cold pack over my ankle before giving me a kind smile and slipping out of the room. The pain meds they gave me are taking the edge off, but my ankle is swollen and puffy. It's got to be broken or something. I've never had an injury like this before, even with all the sports I've played over the years.

Stupid loose rocks. They turned my ankle when I wasn't looking and then sent me flying down that hill.

"Where's Beck?" I murmur to Bianca, who hasn't left my side this entire time.

"Probably pacing the waiting room."

I close my eyes, resting back on the pillows and feeling kind of sick.

Exhaustion is smothering me. "What a mess."

"I'm just glad you're okay. I was so worried about you." Bianca slips her fingers into the palm of my hand.

I give them a gentle squeeze and try to smile at her. "I'm sorry to put you through that. I didn't mean to get lost. I mean, I wasn't really lost, but I slipped on these rocks and ended up tumbling down a hill. Hayden caught me, and then we were both too injured to get very far."

"Why were you out there?"

I peek my eyes open to glance at her, then shut them tight again. "Hayden and I had a fight. He stormed off, and I left it too long to go find him. He got lost and…" I shrug. For some reason I suddenly feel like crying again. It's like the whole thing is landing on top of me, a great boulder that's squishing the life out of me. "I was so scared I'd never see him again. Things could have gone so differently tonight." My voice wobbles.

"But they didn't." Bianca kisses my forehead. "You found him, and you're both alive and safe."

I swallow, tears burning behind my eyelids. "He saved my life tonight. He caught me and held on when I could have fallen in the river. He hurt himself to protect me."

"That's because he's your window," Bianca whispers.

"What?"

"Hayden's your window."

I crack my eyes open and frown at Bianca. It's hard to see her with these tears blurring my vision. "My what?"

"It's just something Missy says. That when life closes a door, God opens a window. Jonas was the door, and Hayden is your window."

I wrinkle my forehead. "You believe in God? After everything we've been through? After losing Mum and Dad and all the shit that's followed?"

"Well…" Bianca looks thoughtful for a moment. "Yeah. I do."

"Why?"

She shrugs, her eyes glistening as she purses her lips, then sniffs. "I hate that Mum and Dad died, and I'd do anything to take it back and have them here with us again. But sometimes… I mean, look at some of the things that have happened. Cam. Missy. The farm. Hanging out with you more. None of that would have happened if they were still here. If we were still living in China."

A tear trickles free, gliding down my cheek. She doesn't bother brushing it away.

"And if Jonas hadn't done what he'd done." Her expression hardens a little. "And don't get me wrong, I *hate* that he did what he did, but if he hadn't, you never would've gone to hide by the caretaker's shed. You wouldn't have met Hayden. You wouldn't have given him a chance or gotten to know him and figured out how incredible he is."

It hurts to swallow. Words are impossible right now, so I just lie there, quietly blinking at my sister.

Bianca's watery eyes glimmer with a smile. "I guess I like to think that... well, that's God's way of showing us that He loves us, that life can still be good even when the worst things happen."

My lips wobble. "I hurt my ankle pretty bad and nearly died tonight. Do you think God could maybe be a little more subtle about it?"

Bianca giggles. "Maybe. But you also figured out that Hayden's everything you want in a guy, right? I mean, the way you were sitting together in the waiting room was... well, super cute."

She's countering every one of my points tonight.

Man, maybe she is right.

I sniff and blink, slashing tears off my face. "He's the last guy I ever thought I'd fall for. I don't get it."

"You don't have to. Sometimes the things we think we want aren't right for us. Hayden cares about you, Stace. Heck, he probably loves you, and I know you've got the big feels for him."

It's impossible to hide my grin.

Hayden loves me?

My heart is singing all of a sudden.

"You're great together."

"I know."

"Really?" Bianca squeezes my hand. "So, you guys *are* like officially together? I can talk about it in front of people and stuff?" She smiles with glee, then puts on a voice. "Yeah, that's my sister and her boyfriend, Hayden. Aren't they cute together?"

"Shut up." I let out a tired laugh, then groan, reaching for my ankle. "How much longer?"

Bianca peeks her head out from the curtain. "Yeah, hi. Excuse me… Hi. My sister's been waiting a really long time. Is the doctor coming back soon?"

"He'll be along shortly," a voice replies. "We're run off our feet tonight, but give me your sister's name and I'll see if I can hurry things along."

I rest my hand on my forehead while Bianca helps me out.

Soon she's back by my side, lightly caressing my hair the way Mom used to. It feels so good, it almost eliminates the pain in my ankle.

"I'm proud of you, Stace. You're an amazing person."

I open my eyes to look up at my sister. Her face is radiating with this affectionate smile.

"Love you, Bee."

She leans forward and kisses my cheek, and I realize just how blessed I am.

Maybe she does have a point about the whole *good can still come out of bad stuff* thing.

Maybe God does exist, and maybe He does love me enough to bring me the things I need.

Hayden's sweet smile swirls through my brain, and I'm overcome with this deep sense of gratitude. Things could have gone so much worse tonight.

But they didn't.

40

HAYDEN

My arm is now locked against my side, but the sling is cutting into my neck. I try to adjust the band and Dad steps forward to help me.

His hands are kind of shaking. I can feel them trembling against the nape of my neck.

I glance up at him.

We haven't said much to each other since he arrived. I've gone through all the painful tests and now know that I've most likely torn some of the ligaments in my shoulder. I have to come back again tomorrow to have this confirmed. For now, I just have to immobilize everything. As for my ribs, the X-rays revealed no cracks or hairline fractures.

"They're just badly bruised," the doctor informed me. "I want you to take it nice and easy for the next week or so. Give yourself a chance to heal."

I nodded, and then he left to go and write my medication script.

As soon as that's done, Dad will take me home. Although, I don't want to leave without seeing Stacey to make sure she's okay.

"That feel better?" Dad steps back, and I nod.

"Thanks."

He shakes his head, and I can feel it coming. The speech I don't want to hear. Holding my breath, I psych myself up to just take it. I don't know if I have the energy to argue or make any kind of point.

"You scared the life out of me, mate." Dad crosses his arms, like he's holding himself together. "When that Bianca girl called me and said you were on the way to the hospital..." He shakes his head and starts pacing. "Lost in the bush?"

"Yeah, I know, Dad. I'm an idiot. I should have known better than to go off trail."

Dad stops walking and looks at me. "Actually, I wasn't going to say that."

"Oh yeah? What were you going to say? Because if it's something about me needing to toughen up or man up or any of that bullshit, I really don't want to hear it." My eyebrows pop high and I blink, rehashing what I just said and wondering where it came from.

What is happening to me right now?

And why aren't I fighting tears as I say this stuff?

I rub my eyes, feeling for moisture, but they're dry.

Dad's face bunches and he starts nibbling the inside of his lip like he's chewing tobacco or something.

I sniff, Stacey's words blooming in my head like bright sunflowers. Sitting up a little straighter, I swallow and look my dad square in the face. "I'm sure Tom or Christian or Maddox would have handled tonight better than I did. I know that's what you're thinking, and I'm sorry you feel like you've been duped getting me as a son. But, you know, I might be different, but that doesn't make me worse. There are lots of different types of men in this world. It would be a complete disaster if we were all blokes like you. Not to mention boring. The world needs variety. People shouldn't have to fit into any particular mold to feel like they're good enough. I'm a *man*, Dad. I may not be able to bench as much as you, and my voice might be higher and, yeah, I cry! But I'm creative and I've got style and I'm romantic. And that doesn't make me any less manly than any other guy out there!"

Dad's a statue now, gaping at me like I've grown a second head while I was talking.

Closing my eyes, I dip my head and am *now* fighting tears. The words that ballooned inside of me seem to be deflating as fast as they appeared, sinking into oblivion before I can capture any more.

My throbbing shoulder reminds me I'm exhausted, and I'm about to whisper, "Can we just go?" when Dad starts talking.

"I, uh…" He swallows, then clears his throat. "You're…" He sighs, and I open my eyes to take in his agonized expression. "Mum always understood you better than I did. When she got sick, I was terrified that I wouldn't know what to do with you. You getting bullied and hurt at school… it killed me. I wanted to make it better, and I thought that teaching you to toughen up would be the ticket. I didn't realize that it was making you feel…" He points at me. "Well… the way you do."

I blink, surprised by the glassy sheen in his eyes.

"I've been floundering ever since she died," Dad says quietly. "I am so underqualified to raise a creative, artistic kid like you. I'm out of my depth, mate." He rubs a hand over his bald head. "But that doesn't mean I don't love you. And I'm not ashamed of you. I just don't know how to help you be… you."

Are Dad's eyes still shimmering?

Did his voice just quake?

Slipping off the bed, I shuffle toward him, feeling small

and skinny the way I always do. With a sniff, I wrap my good arm around his waist and rest my head on his shoulder.

"You don't have to do that, Dad. I can figure out how to be me. You just… You've just got to accept me for who I am, and don't try to change me."

Dad's burly arm locks around me so tight I let out an involuntary squeak.

"Sorry, mate. Sorry." He steps back, his arms lifting like he's worried he might break me.

I smile at him.

He catches my expression and lets out a dry chuckle, lightly pinching my chin.

I can tell by the expression on his face that he loves me, and is maybe even proud of me.

What do you know? Miracles *are* real.

Blinking at my tears, I sniff and rasp, "I love you too, by the way."

"Yeah, I know. Even though I drive you nuts, I'll always be your dad, and I'm proud that you'll always be my son."

Wow.

My chest is suddenly filled with bubbles, and I can't

help a smile as I hold out my fist. He pounds his knuckles against mine before pulling me into another hug. This time I manage to stifle my squeak. This embrace is worth the pain.

41

WILLOW

We've been home for a little while now.

Harper has cleaned my wound for the second time now and re-bandaged it. I'm sitting on the couch in the living room, nursing a milo while Harper calls to check in with Beck.

My leg is perched on April's lap, and she's softly humming between sips of her drink.

"How are you feeling?" she asks, resting her hand on my knee.

"Yeah, okay." I shrug. "It hurts, but it's not too bad. The Panadol must be kicking in." I purse my lips and look over my shoulder to make sure Harper's not listening. Tane's upstairs trying to settle Oscar and Mike, which is turning out to be quite the mission. "Do you think I should let Heath know?"

April shakes her head. "It's not like he can come over here or anything. That'd blow the whole secret relationship out of the water."

"True." I slump back against the couch, wondering why the secret relationship doesn't feel so enticing tonight. It's usually such a thrill to think I'm dating an older guy no one knows about.

An older fulla.

Manu's voice pierces me, and I can't help a touch of sadness. Maybe that's why he's so wary of Heath, because his mum got burned by an older guy.

But Heath isn't Manu's dad. I don't know what that man was like, but Heath loves me. He wouldn't knock me up and abandon me.

Besides, we use protection. We're fine. I'm not about to get pregnant. I'm fifteen, for crying out loud.

I rub at the anxious jitterbugs in my stomach. They're probably just harassing me because I'm tired. It's been a harrowing evening.

"Manu took good care of you tonight," April murmurs, glancing at me sideways and biting the edge of her lip. "You should be with someone like him."

"What?" I tip my head, wondering if I heard her right.

April's face crumples. "That's why I took off with Cam and Bee, so you could spend some time with him. You say you want reckless and exciting. I see that in Moo, but he's got the added advantage of a good heart."

"What are you doing?" I move my leg off her lap and shift it to the coffee table. "Are you trying to set me up with Manu?"

"No." April cringes. "Yes. Maybe. I know you're with Heath. I know you love him and everything, but he's not a good guy."

"He's your brother. You shouldn't say that about him."

"You don't know what he's like, Will. Not really. He's only shown you his good side so far."

I swallow, too nervous to ask what April really means about his good side, and obviously implying that he's got a really bad side too. Have I glimpsed it already?

No. He bought me chocolates. He made it right.

Crossing my arms, I ignore the pounding in my chest.

"I'm just worried about you. I want you to get out while you still can."

"What does that even mean? While I still can?"

"If you'd just told me when you first started seeing him, I could have warned you away. But by the time I found out, he already had his hooks in you."

I frown. "He doesn't have his hooks in me. It's not like that. We *love* each other."

April looks pained and a little desperate. "Is it really love, Will?"

"Yes," I say firmly. "It really is."

April dips her head as Harper comes over. I seal my lips, my heart pumping wildly. I don't understand why it won't slow down.

"Everything's okay. Hayden's gone home with his dad, and Stacey's got a hairline fracture in her talus, so they're fixing her with a moon boot and then Beck will bring her and Bee home for the night."

"Have Manu and Cam made it home all right?"

Why am I asking that?

"Yep. Cam dropped Moo home, and then he's gone back to his place for the night. But he'll join us for the camp pack-up tomorrow." Harper gives me a stern look. "You will not be coming. You need to rest your leg."

I nod, too tired to argue with her.

Harper runs a hand down her face, looking pale and exhausted. "What a day."

April smiles at her. "It's all worked out okay in the end."

"Yeah." Harper nods, obviously appreciating the sentiment. "I'll go set up the airbed in our room. It'll be squishy, but we can all fit."

April thanks her and looks at me while Harper heads upstairs.

Taking my hand, she squeezes my fingers and doesn't say anything else.

Our conversation about Heath is obviously over, so it's weird that I can't shake this ugly foreboding in my chest.

I rub at the annoyance, but it sticks around, lingering like a bad smell.

By Tuesday, the sensation has definitely eased. Life is getting back to normal, and Stacey is only being a slight pain in the ass hobbling around in her moon boot. She's seriously not the world's best patient.

Although Harper just told me I wasn't either as we argued our way to ballet.

I've basically insisted that I have to go. She has no idea I won't be dancing, but I promised her that if it hurt, I'd call her for an early pickup.

"Or I'll just sit to the side and watch the end of the lesson."

"Promise that you will." Harper's sounding all mother-ish, and it's annoying me.

"I will!" I keep my gaze focused on the window, not wanting to look her in the face as I lie to her.

Heath's expecting me. He hasn't seen me since Thursday, and I don't want to let him down. I'm also hoping that just seeing his face will eradicate the uneasiness completely. He'll hold me and remind me that he loves me, and all will be right with the world again.

No more doubts.

No more fleeting thoughts of Manu.

As soon as Harper pulls up to the curb, I jump out and wave goodbye. She lingers, forcing me to walk all the way up to the old church door before finally driving off. The white station wagon disappears down the street, and I run back down the stairs and around the side of the building.

Heath's there waiting for me, a massive smile on his face as I run toward him. Just like in a movie, he gathers me up, holding me tight against his solid chest before kissing me hotly on the mouth.

My body trembles as he drags me around to his car. He drives to a quiet spot, talking about his weekend the whole time. He went to a couple of parties and watched some sports game. I kind of tune out, because all I can think is *Surely April told him I hurt my leg. Why isn't he checking that I'm okay?*

It's so different from Manu. He especially came by to

see me on Sunday. He helped Cam and the guys pack down the campsite, then asked to come back to the farmhouse. He found me in my room, poking his head in quickly to check on my leg.

"You right, ballerina girl?"

"Yeah." I was smiling before I even realized it.

He did his melodic giggle and wiggled his eyebrows. "Not gunna let some little cut stop you from doing the twirly things, right?"

I lost my voice then, but thankfully my smile stayed in place until he waved goodbye and disappeared out my door.

It was kind of sweet, and I keep thinking about it for some weird reason.

"You listening?" Heath frowns at me.

I blink and force a smile. "Of course. So, who won?"

He goes into more details of the game, and I remind myself that Heath not checking on me is fine. I don't want to talk about my leg anyway. I don't want to tell him about the camping trip or some of the stuff I spilled to April and Moo. It's awkward, and I don't feel comfortable baring my soul like that.

Heath probably doesn't want to hear it anyway.

I push Manu's little grin out of my head and focus back on Heath when he parks the car near the hiking trail we took last time. I'll need to be more careful as we tramp through the bush this time. He cuts the engine and turns to look at me. He's drinking me in like I'm beautiful, and it's hard not to smile beneath his adoring gaze

"I've missed you," he whispers, lightly touching my face.

My smile grows a little wider.

"Come on." He gets out of the car and grabs some things from the boot, including a blanket and picnic basket.

"Wanted to make it special." He wiggles his eyebrows, and I follow him to the secluded spot off the trail. Our shoes crunch over sticks and rocks. I make sure to watch my footing, not wanting another spill. My shin still kind of hurts a little. Thankfully, it's protected by a bandage.

Heath flicks out the blanket, settling down and producing a beer and a vodka mixer out of the cooler.

"Thanks." I guzzle some quickly, needing the liquor to help me relax.

I don't know why I'm so jittery. This is Heath. My boyfriend.

He leans toward me, his lips trailing a line from my earlobe and down to my breasts.

Here we go.

This is why I need the liquor. I clench my jaw, wondering if I have the courage to tell him I'm not really in the mood.

But he'll be expecting this. I don't want him to get all pissy again.

His lips work their way back up to mine and he kisses me hard, tipping my body back so he can lie on top of me.

"I don't want you to leave me again." He pulls back, gazing down at my face. "It sucked not having you around." His smile goes soft and he gently kisses my cheek, weaving his fingers into my hair. "We'll be together forever."

I search his face, not sure what to say.

"Right, Will?"

I try for a smile but wonder what my quivering lips are really doing.

"Say it." His blue eyes glint, the words sounding harsher than he probably means them to be. "Say we'll be together forever."

I open my mouth, but it's dry and nothing's coming out.

His fingers curl a little tighter into my hair. It's starting to hurt, and my eyes water at the sting.

"Ow," I mouth.

His grip is unrelenting, tugging at my hair as he leans right over my face and whispers against my cheek, "I need to hear you say it, Willow."

I swallow, hissing as he tugs a little harder. "We will." I suck in a sharp breath. "We'll be together forever."

His grip loosens instantly, a smile spreading across his face. The glint in his eye has disappeared, and it's almost like looking at a different person. The one who first captured me.

He kisses my lips, his tongue thrusting into my mouth like he's claiming ownership of me. With efficient hands, he rids me of my clothes, and I somehow feel powerless to stop it.

It's kind of like drowning. As I lie beneath Heath, letting him take me, I can't help thinking of April's warning.

"You don't know what he's like. You've only seen his good side."

Did I just glimpse Heath's dark side?

Fear coils in my stomach, my mind going numb as Heath pants in my ear and I'm smothered by an overwhelming dread.

42

STACEY

I t's Willow's sixteenth birthday tomorrow.
I can't believe it.

Two weeks just disappeared like that. We're having a small party for her at the farmhouse, and then two days later, school goes back.

In spite of the moon boot, it's been a pretty decent two weeks. Most of it has been at either Hayden's house or mine, depending on who can give us a lift where. Shelley—the total romantic—has been going out of her way to help us out. I love that she loves us.

She even set us up on this really amazing date. I felt like a total grown-up, dressing up and going to this fancy restaurant in town. She had a two-for-one voucher and gave it to Hayden. We sat in that restaurant for hours, sharing each course, critiquing each item on the plate and talking the entire time. The waiter actually had to ask us to leave because they wanted to close up for the night.

Classic!

We've decided to officially dub that as our first date and just forget about that one in the Hamilton Gardens. If that's the case, then Hayden and I celebrating our one-week anniversary at the mall, birthday present shopping for Willow.

His fingers are threaded between mine as we amble slowly through the shops. I can't do much else with this stupid moon boot, and I'm going to have to sit down soon because my leg is starting to ache. Beck keeps telling me off for overusing it.

"Just because you've got that on doesn't mean you can just walk around everywhere."

"I basically spent the first week bedridden," I argued. "I'm going out of my mind!"

"You've made up for it this week, believe me. Now stop pushing so hard and take it easy!" We huffed in each other's faces before he got to do the spin and storm off. I had to hobble to the couch and slump down while Bianca and Cam fought their smiles.

"Shut up! Both of you," I grumbled, which just set them off with the giggles.

Thank God Hayden arrived a few minutes later. He came bearing a beautiful bunch of lavender, which made me think of Mum. Both Bianca and I teared up, and I had the privilege of thanking the sweetest guy on the planet with a kiss before he propped my moon boot onto his lap and picked a romantic movie for us to watch.

"Hey, fancy a Tank juice?" Hayden squeezes my hand, bringing me back to the present.

"You read my mind." I smile at him. "I'll go for a Pineapple Paradise, please. The biggest cup you can get me." Taking a seat at a table on the outskirts of the food court, I hand him a twenty-dollar bill. "Grab yourself something too."

He grins and takes the money, but I know what he's going to do. He'll return with two drinks and a twenty-dollar bill. It's sweet that he wants to pay for everything, but I can't keep letting him do it.

I wonder if I should take *him* out on a date.

My eyes narrow as an idea sparks in my brain, images of me surprising him. I'll have to call Shelley and get her on board. She'll be totally into it.

I just need to come up with something Hayden will love, which won't be too hard because we basically love all the same stuff, except sport. He's not that into it, which is fine. Bianca assured me the other night when I was lying awake worrying about it that you can't have *everything* in common.

Pulling out my phone, I start texting Shelley but have to stop quickly as Hayden returns. I don't want him to know what I'm up to.

Slipping my phone into my bag, I grin as he places the drink in my hand, the twenty bucks on the table, and his mouth on my lips.

"Thank you."

"My pleasure." He eases into a chair, careful of his shoulder, which is still in a sling. He sucks on his cardboard straw and wiggles his eyebrows at me.

I laugh and lean across the table for another kiss, just as a group of North Ridge High girls wander past us.

"Stacey!" Luka jolts to a stop, her eyes bulging when she sees what I'm about to do.

"Oh, hey, Luka." I smile, my heart taking off like someone just shouted, *"Ready, set, go!"*

She's with Melina and Kim, and all three of them are eyeing me with curiosity. I glance at Hayden, who gives me an edgy little grin.

I guess this is our first test in public... and it's up to me to pass it.

"Hey, you guys know Hayden, right?"

They look at him and nod, Luka's eyes shooting back to mine, silently asking the question they're all desperately wanting the answer to.

I look across the table again. Hayden gives me another tight smile, and I know this is my do-or-die moment. We've talked about the return to school, and he understands completely about why I wanted to keep things between us on the down-low. The Jonas thing is huge, but… you know what?

"We're celebrating our one-week anniversary."

I hold my cup up and Hayden does the same, looking completely shocked by my admission. I tap our drinks together and then suck on my straw.

"Wow." Luka forces a smile. "How'd you… um…" She tips her head and then points to my moon boot. "What happened?"

"Oh, camping trip went a little wrong, but then…" I smile across the table at Hayden. "A whole lot went right too."

He gives me a gooey smile, and my heart does this giddy jumpy thing.

The girls are all exchanging awkward glances, but then Melina's mouth busts into a wide grin. "I want to hear that story. I always love knowing how couples got together."

I raise my eyebrows at Hayden. He snickers and grins. "Maybe we'll tell you sometime."

Melina smiles, then nudges Kim and Luka. "Come on, you guys. Let them enjoy their date."

"See you at school." I wiggle my fingers and they trail after her, still looking over their shoulders a couple of times like they can't quite believe it.

"Well, the whole school should know about us by Monday morning," I murmur, raising my eyebrows at him.

"Why'd you do that?" He shakes his head. "I thought we were keeping us quiet."

"Yeah." I wrinkle my nose. "But that'll be such a pain in the ass. Secret relationships always lead to complications, and I just want to be myself and not have to hide or pretend at school."

Hayden looks suitably impressed.

I smirk as I raise my right eyebrow at him. "I'm just figuring out who I want to be." I wink at him and take another sip of the juicy sweet drink.

"I'm proud of you." He grins.

"And I'm proud of my man, so that's why I'm claiming him."

He tips his head back with an ecstatic moan. "Aw, say that part again."

I giggle. "I'm claiming you?"

"No, the *my man* part."

I smile and lean across the table, whispering, "My

man," before kissing him on the lips.

He really is a great kisser. Our chairs squeak on the shiny floor as we tug them a little closer so we can make out in the middle of the mall with people milling around us.

I'm not ashamed to be head over heels for Hayden Thorp.

Girls like Luka may raise their eyebrows, but she doesn't know.

See, I'm the lucky one.

I got the guy who knows how to treat me right. He loves me, makes me laugh, and he's the world's best friend.

I scored a keeper, and I have no intention of ever letting him go again.

Keep reading to find out what's going to happen next to the Connell family.

Willow's caught in a relationship she's too afraid to get out of, and things are only getting worse as Heath's dark side shows itself more readily each time they're together.

Manu knows something is up with the ballerina girl

and can't shake the feeling that she's in trouble. One night, he sees the truth, but will his bid to save her end in disaster?

The Connell crew are about to get rocked to the core as a horrific accident exposes dark truths and hidden secrets.

FRACTURED GIRL vs RECKLESS BOY
Releasing March 6, 2020

She's trapped in an abusive relationship. He's determined to set her free. Will love give her the courage to let him?

Willow:

I didn't see Heath's dark side until it was too late.

Now he's never going to let me go.

He won't even let me talk to other guys, especially not Manu.

But Manu wants to be my friend.

He keeps being so nice to me and I keep letting him, because… well, maybe he's the one I truly want.

I don't know how I'm going to get out of this.

I'm terrified, and I can't tell anybody the truth.

I wish my dad was still alive. He'd save me from this nightmare.

Now I have no one.

Or do I?

Manu suspects something is up. Is it safe to let him in?

Or am I just exposing us both to a raging storm we can't outrun?

Fractured Girl vs Reckless Boy is the sixth story in the emotionally charged Forever Love YA contemporary romance series. If you like heart-wrenching love stories filled with raw emotion and thrilling drama, then you'll love Jordan Ford's breathtaking romance.

Buy Fractured Girl vs Reckless Boy to see love shine through the darkest fear today!

PREVIEW

FRACTURE GIRL VS WOUNDED BOY

MANU

Willow's lips curl into a smile that does something funny to my chest.

I swallow, weirded out by it. But she's still looking at me, so I need to say something.

"Happy birthday for Friday. Heard you had a party."

She nods and glances at the shelves in front of her. Rows of healthy snacks—nuts, dried fruit, mini pretzels.

"You have a good time?"

"Yeah. Thank you." She shrugs, gliding towards me. "It wasn't really a party, though. I mean is was just family and April… and Cam and Hayden. They seem to kind of be family now."

I keep my smile in place, trying not to feel the intense tug of jealousy. I'd do anything to become part of a family like that. Clearing my throat, I point at the shelf she was just looking at. "You buying some nuts?"

She gives a sad snicker. "Thinking about it. Just want a snack, while I wait for..." Her voice trails off and my stomach pinches. The look on her face... what does it mean?

Something's eating at her. I wish I could ask, but that's kinda rude, right? Like you shouldn't really get up in people's faces with your curiosity. Mum's told me off so many times for asking the wrong questions.

"It's rude to poke around in people's personal stuff, Manu. Just keep your mouth shut."

I wiggle my eyebrows at her, trying to make her feel better. "You can hang with me if you like. Stack some shelves."

I get the desired effect of a smile, but it doesn't stay on her face very long.

What does that look in her eyes mean?

"Hey, you all right?"

She hesitates, then looks away from me. "Yeah. Yeah, I'm good. I'm *all* good."

Not.

Screw keeping my mouth shut.

I narrow my eyes at her, closing the fridge and leaning my shoulder against the cold glass. "You sure?"

Her forehead wrinkles and she looks at me, her eyes suddenly glassing over.

I stand up and move towards her. "What's the matter?"

"Did you know Tane and Harper were together?"

TANE

Harper's pacing around the garage like a caged tiger. It's painful to watch and I wish there was something I could say to soothe her. Her agitation is palpable.

"It's going to be okay," I murmur again.

"Would you stop saying that!" Her slender arms fly out like wings. "Willow is pissed!"

"Maybe." I lean against the pool table, careful to keep my tone light. "I think she's more surprised than anything, though."

She whips around to face me, raising her finger before I can say anything else. "Don't start. I know exactly what you're going to say."

Crossing my arms, I study her expression and softly ask, "What's that?"

"You're going to say that we should have told every-body, or it's about time we tell everybody!"

I stretch my arms wide. "So? Shouldn't we?"

"No!"

"Why not?"

"Because!"

I tip my head to the side, hoping my expression is droll enough. "That's not an answer."

With a sharp sigh, she paces away from me, running her long fingers through her luscious hair. "I'm not ready."

"Basically everyone already knows now."

"Not Oscar! Not Beck!" She points towards the house. "They will freak out!"

"And it'll only be worse if we don't come forward and tell them first. The longer we're together, the more awkward it is that we've kept everyone in the dark? Why can't we just come out and tell everyone?"

I push off the table and get within range, reaching out to gently pull her to a stop when she paces past me.

"Don't," she mutters, but I ignore her terse comment and guide her into my arms.

Her stiff body soon relaxes, melding against mine. I cup

the back of her head and brush my lips across her forehead.

"I know you're worried about how this might effect everyone, but I love you, Harp. And I'm proud of that. I'm not afraid of anyone's reaction. Because whether they're happy, sad, annoyed, indifferent, it doesn't matter. Nothing anyone can say will change how I feel about you. So let's just tell everyone."

She goes stiff again, wriggling out of my embrace. Her smile is strained and it makes my heart sink. What's she not saying to me right now?

HARPER

Crap! Why did Dylan have to text me now. Especially with a photo of him standing in front of the pyramids with a big *"WISH YOU WERE HERE!"* underneath it.

This is the last thing I need.

And now Tane's eyes are all narrowed and he's staring suspiciously at me.

What do I say?

He gets so immature and pissy when he knows I've been texting Dylan. It annoys the heck out of me. His jealousy is stupid. I'm with *him,* and staying in touch with my ex in a friendly, unromantic way is not cheating! Tane needs to get over himself, but with the tension already frothing between us, I can't exactly say that.

"It's nothing," I murmur.

He huffs and shakes his head. "It's not nothing. I can see your face right now, you know."

I roll my eyes, so not wanting to get into this. Agitation over how I'm going to solve this Willow problem is eating me alive and now I have to deal with Tane too.

Snapping my eyes shut, I wish for a moment that I was Dorothy, and I could just tap my ruby slippers together and magically appear back in Wellington with my friends. I could be sitting on a couch right now, eating popcorn and watching romantic TV shows with them!

It'd be so easy and simple and uncomplicated.

"Harp?"

Tane's voice pulls me back to reality and I creep my eyes open to look at him.

Do I lie?

No! Haven't you done enough of that for one day?

Guilt over not telling Willow punches the words out of me. "It's Dylan." I point to the phone in my pocket. "He's in Egypt right now and sent me a photo of him standing in front of the pyramids. One of those trick ones where he's holding one of the pyramids in his hand, you know?"

Should I pull out my phone and show him?

The look on Tane's face right now is telling me... nope!

WILLOW

"Willow!" Heath slams the brake, so I jerk forward in my seat. The seat belt catches me hard against the chest and I gasp as he pulls to the side of the road. Snatching my chin, he forces me to look at him. "Do you love me or not?"

His fierce glare forces the words out of me. "Of course I love you."

"Then don't torture me by hanging out with that guy. I'll go crazy if I'm picturing you hanging out with him at school all day. April's your school friend. You stick with her." His expression gentles, but not his pinch on my chin. He squeezes a little harder, his blue eyes glinting. "Okay?"

I swallow and blink, then when he lets me go, I force myself to nod. Rubbing my tender chin with trembling fingers, I try to smile at him.

He grins back and I'm suddenly looking at a completely different person—the sweet, suave guy I fell for a few months ago. His eyes are bright and beaming, the lines of his face taking on a gentle edge.

Cupping my cheek like I'm a delicate flower petal, he leans forward and pecks my lips.

"Good," he whispers. "You know, it's times like this, I wish we could go public so everyone knows you're mine."

He pulls me in for another kiss, this one heated and demanding. I meet his tongue with my own, knowing it's what he wants.

The word *mine* continues to ring in my head over and over.

Mine. I used to swoon at the sound of that.

I was his.

His girl.

His love.

MINE!

Now it's a clanging gong in my brain.

I don't feel cherished anymore.

I'm starting to feel owned.

Fractured Girl vs Reckless Boy is available on Amazon.

Made in the USA
Las Vegas, NV
04 January 2022

40396872R00210